What People Are Saying About

Recognitions: a novel

Think *Cloud Atlas*, a classic story of rebirth, many lives, and reincarnation on a level that involves protagonists in other lives – but take it a step further in *Recognitions*, the first novel in a trilogy, which presents a woman under hypnosis who sometimes encounters a French girl on the cusp of marriage and sometimes an African shaman facing a village's struggles with illness and slavery.

Then take these diverse li⸱ ⸱ together in the story of a modern-day woma⸱ ⸱h these other lives and her own daily ⸱uggle to understand the connection⸱ ⸱eams and hypnotic state), and you have an ⸱aga filled with three threads that lead back to one ta⸱ ⸱nder.

Under a differen⸱ ⸱.and, this saga of birth, death, and afterlife could have easily proved confusing: it's no simple matter to create three disparate, very different lives, and weave them together with purpose and discovery; no easy venture to bring all these pieces to life and then meld them into one.

It's also satisfying to note that the protagonist doesn't just skip into acceptance of these threads and their impact on her life; she's pulled in reluctantly and initially believes these results from hypnotherapy and dream states to be 'craziness'. She's no new-age believer: she's a wife, mother, and has a life of her own: "I hardly have time to explore all sorts of strange mind-body-spirit connections or whatever they call them these days."

But it's a life destined to transform (though her husband's departure has already started the process of vast changes) in unexpected ways, and the gift here lies in how past, present, and future worlds not only connect, but collide.

There are many passages that support all kinds of emotional connections and disconnects, as well: "But I resolved to call Don later and tell him that there's something going on with our daughter. I'll call him even if talking to him will make me feel emotional, anxious, and envious of the quick fix he'd found in his life. Even if it would make me feel betrayed and confused by my feelings towards him – how his cynicism annoyed me for years, how I couldn't stand his macho jokes anymore and how relieved I had first felt when we decided to separate. We said we'd remain friends, for the kids' sakes. We said we'd see how it would go if we just parted amicably for a while, and then take it from there."

As Amelia's life changes and as her novel-writing is spiced by her dream states, she finds the courage to not only probe these events, but understand and incorporate them into her own world: "I needed to visit this place. This would help me understand more about Adele's world, it would be research, not some craziness destined to satisfy my sudden and illogical fascination with past lives, I said to myself."

The result (much like *Cloud Atlas*'s ability to make readers think far past the last page) is a story that is quietly compelling: a moving saga highly recommended for any reader interested in predetermination, past lives, and how three disparate worlds weave together.

Diane Donovan, Midwest Book Review

Recognitions centers on Amelia, who, under hypnosis and in dreams, sometimes encounters an intelligent French girl on the verge of choosing a future husband and sometimes an African shaman trying to save his village from sickness and slavery. As she struggles to understand her connection to these two people, her everyday relationships carry on with an ex-husband and two teenage children. When a man from her past comes into the picture and introduces her to fencing, the connections begin to click.

Daniela I. Norris writes in clean, sparse prose, so she is able to paint the picture of three lives on three different continents with distinct voices for each without ever resorting to gratuitous description. As a result, the book moves at a fast pace, but without feeling rushed or empty. And even though I wanted to know how it would play out, I didn't skip a single

word because every word was relevant in this engaging story.
Lorelai Rivers, Readers' Favorite

A delightfully written book that will captivate the reader.
Andy Tomlinson author of *Healing the Eternal Soul*

Daniela Norris has created a skilled interweaving of stories in her debut novel *Recognitions*, revealing connections across time, place, gender, language, age, and race. Through her contemporary protagonist Amelia, a foreign rights book editor in New York whose failed marriage and role as single mother of teens present very specific challenges, the reader also experiences the life stories of a revered African shaman and a 17th-century French girl entering adulthood.

The details are vivid and illuminating, and certainly more than the stuff of dreams and coincidences. Discovering Amelia's experience with hypnosis and past-life regression leaves the reader comforted, lifted, and intrigued, just like she is. *Recognitions* is a satisfying and remarkably down-to-earth exploration of the hazy spectrum from fact to fiction to fantasy...and back again.
Nancy Freund, author of *Mailbox: A Scattershot Novel of Racing, Dares and Danger, Occasional Nakedness, and Faith*

This enjoyable and easily read novel is a subtle weave of three plot-lines across four centuries, effortlessly moving between modern-day New York, the seventeenth century Franco Swiss border and finally, an African village entering the trauma of the colonial age. The main protagonist is the New Yorker Amelia – author, mother, recent divorcee – who begins the story as a broken and jaded character, who in a fit of desperation tries hypnotherapy to regain her lost spark. The hypnotic session unlocks something deep within her psyche, producing vivid dreams or (are they?) recollections; firstly the life of a young peasant girl on the cusp of womanhood, then later an African shaman.

Amelia is never sure if these experiences are excerpts from past lives or just the by-product of an overactive imagination. Nevertheless, she draws great strength and inspiration from these encounters, drawing parallels with her current life and its challenges. It's the author's attention to small details that sells the story, whether describing the excitement of a French girl visiting a shop to buy materials for a new dress, or the intricacies of fencing, or the world of African mysticism. Sympathetic descriptions define well rounded characters and the deeper you get into the story, the more you want to reach its denouement.

Recognitions is a satisfying and thoughtful novel from an experienced author.

R.J. Dearden, author of *The Realignment Case*

On Dragonfly Wings: A Skeptic's Journey to Mediumship

Based on the experiences of the author, upon the untimely death of her brother, it is a well-written and engaging story with plenty of evidence to give comfort to the bereaved.

Editor's Note, Kindred Spirit Magazine May-June 2014

Daniela Norris takes the reader, with warmth and grace, into the discovery of another reality.

Susan Tiberghien, author of *Side by Side: Writing Your Love Story* and *Footsteps: In Love with a Frenchman*

A delightful book that you will find hard to put down once you start to read.

Andy Tomlinson, author of *Healing the Eternal Soul* and *Exploring the Eternal Soul*

On Dragonfly Wings is a book that people who have been through such painful journey would easily identify with. And for those who haven't, this book will open their eyes. The book raises a lot of questions which discerning readers will take time to address.

Khamneithang Vaiphei , Yogi Times

The autobiographical account of a bereavement and how that experience led Daniela to harness her mediumistic gift and to gain meaningful contacts with the unseen worlds.

The Inner Light, Vol 35 No 1

I'm a retired Episcopalian priest and skeptic to most things paranormal. Daniela's descriptions of her "sixth sense" experiences are most effective in helping me continue to balance my perceptions of the material and spiritual realms. My training in religion and lifelong experience of ministry (as both pastor and chaplain), did not relieve me of fear and confusion around death. Then one day I had what I can only call a touch of grace that led me to a life transformation. Thirty years later, I had a stroke and Near Death Experience (NDE) wherein I lost all fear of death and tasted of the ineffable experience of the "Presence". Since then, I have been studying sixth-sense research and reported experiences. Thousands of responsible studies and reports have resulted from the last 200 years of science and experience all over the world. Reports such as Daniela's anecdotes are the most exciting and convincing. Well-written and a delight to read.

David R. Powell

Collecting Feathers: Tales from the Other Side

Like an interesting doorway into a secret inner garden, Daniela Norris' stories invite you into a rich experience of strange and fascinating personal culture. Before you know it, you find yourself on the other side of familiar boundaries of this life and what is beyond.

Mark Perry, CCHT, C-NLP – educator, healer, life fulfillment coach and host of 'A Matter of the Mind' radio show.

Most of us know 'life on the other side' only as a phrase. Daniela Norris shows considerable experience of this mysterious dimension, and shares it through her characters' everyday existences. The naturalness of her viewpoint captivates and she never blinks.

Wallis Wilde-Menozzi, author of *Toscanelli's Ray, a novel*

Daniela Norris is a writer of subtle intelligence. While her stories seldom have a twist, each tale has the power to wriggle from under the readers' expectations.
Jason Donald, author of *Choke Chain, a novel*

The names may change, the story details differ, but family ties and loyalty remain stronger than death and 'truth is beyond words'.
Gwyneth Box, Poet and Poetry Coordinator, SWWJ

Birth, death, afterbirth and afterlife are all intricately wound together against the backdrop of tragedies happening daily and how people cope, move on, and move outward.

That's the living, breathing, beating heart of *Collecting Feathers*, especially recommended not for those who expect entertainment from their short stories, but for readers more interested in reflective pieces spiced with poetic imagery and succinct (but striking) revelations.
Diane Donovan, Midwest Book Review

Collecting Feathers: Tales from the Other Side is a woven text of people, places and tales that try to imitate real life; yet with a fresh viewpoint that changes slightly with each story. The result is a beautiful and varied piece of work. It is vital reading for any curious mind that wants to be taken to new and inventive places.
Sarah Gonnet, www.sabotagereviews.com

Collecting Feathers transports us to a world where our mental barriers and overly constructed stories no longer reduce our existence. It opens a door to another dimension where imagination and reality collide, liberating us from our self-inflicted limitations. Daniela Norris exposes gracefully in this brief but powerful collection of short stories, how we are all connected, and how without judgment, evaluation, or labels, we are capable of accessing the greatest power of our Universe.
Sophie Parienti, Founder & Editor in Chief, Yogi Times.

Recognitions

a novel

Recognitions

a novel

Daniela I. Norris

Winchester, UK
Washington, USA

First published by Roundfire Books, 2016
Roundfire Books is an imprint of John Hunt Publishing Ltd., Laurel House, Station Approach,
Alresford, Hants, SO24 9JH, UK
office1@jhpbooks.net
www.johnhuntpublishing.com
www.roundfire-books.com

For distributor details and how to order please visit the 'Ordering' section on our website.

Text copyright: Daniela I. Norris 2015

ISBN: 978 1 78535 197 6
Library of Congress Control Number: 2015943101

A CIP catalogue record for this book is available from the British Library.

Design: Stuart Davies

Printed and bound by CPI Group (UK) Ltd, Croydon, CR0 4YY, UK

We operate a distinctive and ethical publishing philosophy in all
areas of our business, from our global network of authors to
production and worldwide distribution.

« Il n'y a que deux puissances au monde, le sabre et l'esprit :
à la longue, le sabre est toujours vaincu par l'esprit. »

"There are only two forces in the world, the sword and the
spirit. In the long run the sword will always be conquered by
the spirit."

Napoleon Bonaparte

For all fencers – to their swords, and to their spirits.

One

I was still considering cancelling it all as I entered through the building's gate and stepped towards the door. I took a couple of deep breaths and looked around for clues, to help me decide whether I should go ahead with this craziness or not. I could hear my own heartbeat, which I thought was a bit weird, as I'd never noticed it before. Not like this, thumping in my ears like a distant drumbeat.

There was no name on the door – just a sticker of a dragonfly, and her initials. It looked as if it were the door to a student's apartment, or to the practice of some dodgy manicurist, certainly not a door to another state of consciousness.

When Lauren, my editorial assistant, first suggested hypnotherapy, I laughed. Lauren is the spiritual type, taking three yoga classes a week and constantly talking about meditation, energies and karma. It isn't that I don't believe in these things. In fact, I don't really know what I believe in, I just know that between my teenage kids and my day job and my attempts at finishing my never-ending novel, I hardly have time to explore all sorts of strange mind-body-spirit connections or whatever they call them these days.

But since Don left I pretty much lost it, in more than one way. I couldn't focus on the books piling up on my desk, silently filling me with guilt for letting them sit there for so long. I was supposed to be spending my days securing foreign rights for American books, mostly working with French-language publishers. But I couldn't do my job properly. I suffered from sudden anxieties during the day, and at night I couldn't sleep. It's not that he broke my heart or anything, it's more like he somehow managed to crack the fragile confidence in humanity that I've managed to maintain over the twenty years of living in New York City.

But I couldn't spend the entire day in front of that door with the stupid dragonfly sticker, so I decided to knock. If she turned out to be some kind of witch with missing front teeth and hair coming out of her ears, I could always make a run for it.

A woman in her late thirties opened the door, and all her teeth were intact. In fact, she had a pleasant smile.

"Come in," she said as she shook my hand, and then signaled towards a coat hanger by the door.

As I took my coat off I felt a knot of anxiety in my throat, but I just swallowed it. There was no way back now. Taking my coat off made me feel vulnerable, as if a dice had been thrown; a decision had been made, one I couldn't go back on anymore. I wasn't used to feeling vulnerable; it was a recent state-of-being that I still didn't wear well.

"So why are you here?" she asked.

I was seated in front of her in a black leather armchair, and noticed that both my hands were clenched into tight fists. I had to choose my words carefully because I didn't want to let the wrong ones out. Even though I didn't know her, even though she was supposed to be able to help me with my fears and my worries and my questions, still – I wanted to make a good impression.

"I came because I can't sleep well," I said. "And I've kind of lost interest in things. I've been working on an historical novel for three years now, and it's not progressing. I also have some…I suppose they're called anxieties. About the future. Also about the past."

I stopped there. I didn't want to sound too neurotic.

"Have you gone through any major life changes recently?" she asked, noting down my words. She stopped writing and looked at me with gentle eyes. I then noticed that she was perhaps somewhat older than I initially thought; at least her eyes seemed old.

So then I had to spill it all out. I told her how Don decided one day he'd had enough and how I was initially relieved he left because by then I'd had enough too. We'd been at each other's throats for years and now that the kids were a little older there was no need to pretend any longer. But when he almost immediately moved in with some woman called Claudette, that's when the anxieties started. What if I had made the wrong choice? Was it too late to change it now? Besides, what kind of name is that, anyway, Claudette? Sounded like some granny from a bad fifties movie.

But Claudette was no granny. I saw her when they came to pick up the kids together one Saturday morning about two months ago, shamelessly sitting in the passenger seat of *our* car, or what used to be our car, not even bothering to come out and introduce herself. She wore a little black halter-top despite the fact it was a cold day, exposing skinny shoulders and a big red pendant of some kind draped around her neck like a hangman's noose. Maybe it was just wishful thinking on my part, but I was more than pleased when Tom and Jen came back and said they didn't like her at all.

"She's trying to be funny," said Jen. "But she isn't."

"Yeah, she tried to bribe us with ice cream as if we were little kids," said Tom. He was now a tall, slim teenager, his voice breaking as he spoke.

But none of that mattered now, for I was lying on the therapist's couch as she started counting backwards in a slow, monotone voice, instructing me to relax, breathe deeply, let go of all my worries and put them in a small imaginary box which – she assured me – I'd be able to pick up mentally when we finished the session. It felt nice knowing that I could put away all my worries for a little while, but then get them back if I wanted to. I was quite attached to my worries and anxieties by then, they even felt comfortable and familiar. I could not help but wonder if I was truly and honestly ready to get rid of them.

Two

If I don't get up now, it might be too late, she thought.

What frightened Adele most was that she could not feel her toes. She could see her feet, tucked into warm brown leather boots which were done up with rough, old laces. But she could hardly move them. They were just not responding to her commands.

She gathered her wool skirt and pushed up on her hands, then on her knees, her fingernails clawing the cold, dusty ground. She grunted, feeling a sudden, jolting pain as the blood started flowing to her legs. Up on her feet now, she took two steps and stumbled, supporting herself on a large rock.

It was late in the afternoon and the skies had started changing from gray-blue to indigo. Adele raised her eyes to the clouds, noticing that they now looked heavier, more pregnant than they did just a few hours ago. It felt as if it would start snowing again soon. A late afternoon in the mountains, in early spring. Yes, of course it could still snow, but she didn't think of that earlier in the day when she stormed out of her house down in the village at the foothills of the Jura.

All she could think about that morning was that it was not fair that she, nearly an adult, was being treated like a child, while her fourteen-year-old brother could come and go as he pleased. He had few chores to tend to, just his studies and then chopping firewood or shoveling snow in winter. Her parents treated him like a prince, while treating her like the housemaid.

Of course she didn't mind helping her mother with the cooking and the cleaning and the sewing, that was her duty after all, she was pulling her own weight like everyone around her. But if she could do what she wanted with a little bit of her time…then it would be more tolerable. But instead of doing what she really wanted to do – which was reading, or roaming the woods by her house and enjoying some time on her own, she was expected to work on her embroidery – which she found not only useless and boring, but also ugly.

Adele took a deep breath and left the safety of the solid rock. She could feel her toes now, but they hurt as if someone had broken them one by one. The late-afternoon breeze made her feel as if she was wearing a mask that prevented her from controlling her expression. She grimaced, forcing her facial muscles to move. She then started walking, step after step, in the direction she had thought was home. Only a few hours earlier, what now seemed like an eternity ago, she had confidently walked up the side of these same foothills of the French Jura mountain range. She remembered how the anger and frustration swelled up in her ribcage and the thoughts exploded in her mind.

She could run away from home, she had thought just a few hours earlier. Yes, she could run away to Paris and find work that would allow her to support herself. She would be part of all the exciting political events she had heard about; she would find friends who were influential and romantic, artists and writers. This would be the real life she was meant to live. She could even become a writer herself. She would be eighteen soon and be able to get away from her boring life and live the exciting life of a city girl. She would be like those glamorous women she'd read about in novels.

Now all her anger was gone, and her previous plans did not feel as if they were such a great idea. What would she do on her own in Paris if she could not even take care of herself in these rural parts she knew so well? Paris. What a ridiculous idea. If she made it home safely…if she made it home safely she would be a better daughter to her parents and not lose her temper so quickly. Her parents were probably so worried about her; they had no idea where she'd gone. She hadn't said a thing before she left, she just grabbed her winter coat and stormed out of the house.

Was she even heading in the right direction? Twilight in this eastern part of France arrived quickly on spring days, like a cat pouncing on a bird. Although the days were getting longer and the sun sent its thin, long fingers through the clouds on some days, other days, like this one, were misty and chilly and wet. Small patches of frost dotted the earth around Adele as she stumbled downhill.

I am not going to cry, I am not going to cry…, she thought. But when she reached her fingers up to touch her cheeks, they were wet. And then she saw something that made her stop and listen. It was a light, a light hovering somewhere down beneath her. A light? Was there someone there? Maybe they had come looking for her…

"Hello!" she called, hardly recognizing her own voice. "Hello, *je suis la*, I am here!"

And then something scratching the rocks, something moving towards her, low on the ground. She couldn't see because of the mist but suddenly something large and hairy and wet sniffed her feet and almost made her jump out of her skin.

She let out a faint cry as her legs gave in on her and she fell on her knees. The creature rubbed itself against her and yelped, and then she realized it was a large dog and started laughing. A dog! A dog! It meant that someone was nearby. She felt huge relief and let her consciousness slip away for a moment, and it was only the dog licking her face that brought her back to the here and now.

"*Viens ici!*" she heard a voice calling and saw the master of the dog emerging out of the mist around her, holding a small lantern.

"*Mademoiselle!*" he called as he approached her, his rough wool coat hovering over her as he kneeled by her side. "Are you all right, *mademoiselle*? What are you doing here on your own?"

She tried to answer but her voice would not obey her. All she could do was shake her head at him.

"Come, let's get you off the ground," he said and tried to lift her. She managed to get up and first reluctantly, but then gratefully, accepted his arm.

"We will take you home, where do you live, *mademoiselle*?"

"Chevry," she said, and as they walked together in the opposite direction from which she'd been heading all this time, she glanced at him sideways, not wanting him to notice her staring. She managed to see that he was older than her but not that old, maybe twenty-something. His fur hat covered his forehead and all she could see was dark eyes and a few strands of brown hair stuck to his forehead. All this time she'd been walking in the wrong direction. How foolish was she, she would have never made it home on her own.

They did not talk during the long descent, as the air around them got darker and crisper and the mist hung over their heads like a ghostly umbrella.

"I can get back home now," she said when they reached the outskirts of her village. "I know where I am now, thank you."

"I will take you to your home," he said in a low, quiet voice that left no room for argument. The dog bounced at their feet like a faithful chaperone and Adele reached down to stroke his head. He licked her hand.

"He isn't very old, is he?" she asked, suddenly feeling the need for conversation. She dreaded the encounter with her parents. What would she say to them? That she took off in a temper tantrum and got lost? Her back ached and her feet still felt as if they had been viciously stomped on. Would they be angry? It would be good to have this stranger with her, at least they would not want to embarrass her in front of him, or so she hoped.

They walked towards her house, at the end of the village, and he now followed closely behind her, keeping a respectable distance. The mutt wagged its tail in enthusiasm, as if this was the greatest adventure he'd ever been on. He made Adele laugh.

"This is my house," she said and pointed to the gray-walled building, its sloping red roof almost black under the thin moon. "Would you like to come in?"

He hesitated.

"I believe you will be fine if I leave you here, *mademoiselle*…"

The front door flew open and her mother stormed out of the house, waving her arms.

"Where were you? We did not know what to think. Your father and brother and Monsieur Montague have all gone out looking for you and…"

Her mother noticed the stranger and stopped in mid-sentence, eyeing him suspiciously.

"Who's this?" she said, as if he wasn't there.

"*Maman*, I am sorry, I got lost…he found me…this is…"

Adele suddenly realized she did not know the man's name.

"*Bonjour, madame.*" The stranger approached her mother and bowed his head. "I believe your daughter took off in the wrong direction and got somewhat lost," he said. "My dog found her and was happy to make a new friend," he added and pointed at the mutt, who now wagged its tail enthusiastically at Adele's mother.

A small smile escaped her previously clenched lips, but she quickly resumed her serious expression.

"Do you have a name, young man?" she asked, and he bowed his head again.

"Jules Badeau, at your service, *madame*. I shall leave you now, for I have a long walk ahead of me, back to Gex…"

"You will come inside and have something to drink before you go, Monsieur Badeau," ordered Adele's mother, walking back towards her house. "My husband will want to thank you when he returns," she added.

Jules Badeau looked at Adele, uncertain how to regard the order he had just received.

"Yes," she said. "You must come in for a few moments."

He nodded in resignation.

"*Reste ici*," he instructed the mutt, who immediately obeyed its master's command and sat, its tail still wagging uncontrollably underneath it.

"I shall accept your kind invitation then, *madame*," he said and followed Adele and her mother into the stone-walled house.

The matronly woman sat him by the log fire and stuck a glass of red wine in his hand.

"I prefer not to drink, *madame*," he said and handed it back.

"Oh," was all Madame Durand said in return. Adele just stared at him. Who was this strange man, who just refused the glass of wine her mother offered him?

She noticed Monsieur Badeau looking around the room, taking in the understated elegance and the small details that made the Durand home pleasant and welcoming. The sofa was well-used but covered with beautiful fabric, small embroidered flowers on the arm-rests. The four chairs around the room were of solid, high-quality cherry-wood.

"Adele, go sit by the fire," came the instruction from the kitchen. "If you become ill, I will have to nurse you to health for days now. Go and warm up."

Adele took a sideways glance at the guest and pulled a chair close to the fire, but not too close to him. They sat in awkward silence, each waiting for the other to speak first.

Madame Durand walked into the room carrying a tray with two bowls of fragrant broth.

"So where did you find this irresponsible girl?" she shot at Monsieur Badeau as she offered him his bowl. He accepted it with gratitude, warming his hands on it.

"*Maman...*" Adele started protesting, but was silenced by a hard look from her mother.

"Up in the mountains, *madame*," he said. "Walking in the opposite direction from her house, I seem to recall."

Madame Durand shook her head and left the room, only to

return a moment later with a blanket, which she threw over her daughter's shoulders.

Adele gave Jules Badeau another sideway glance and saw a kind face. Not handsome, not striking, but there was something soft and gentle in the angle he held his chin, as if listening to some inner voice and wondering at what he was hearing.

"And you, *monsieur*, where are you from? I am quite certain I have seen you before, but I cannot say where," Adele's mother asked Monsieur Badeau. He smiled obligingly at the older lady, and then at her daughter, as if saying – *This is not a problem, I can handle it.*

"I was born in a small village near Lyon, *madame*. But I now live in Gex. I teach at a private home there."

Madame Durand's eyes lit up.

"Oh, yes, of course. The new schoolteacher from Gex. Madame Montague talked about you a while back. We saw you at the market a few weeks ago, didn't we? So you have left Lyon to come here and teach?"

"Indeed, *madame*, I have been offered a position in Gex and moved here a month ago. I only lived in Lyon a few years, while I studied."

Adele started shaking under her blanket.

"*O la la*, you have a fever," said her mother, placing her lips on Adele's forehead. "Let's get you into bed with a hot drink."

Monsieur Badeau stood up and was about to excuse himself when the front door opened and Adele's father stormed in, accompanied by his teenage son and the neighbor, Monsieur Montague.

"There you are," he called at Adele, furious. "What happened? Who is this man?"

He pointed at Monsieur Badeau as if he was something the cat had just dragged in.

"*Papa*—" Adele started in a weak voice, but her mother inter-rupted.

"Jean, we will talk of this later. I am taking her to bed now. This is Monsieur Badeau, the schoolteacher from Gex, who found her wandering up in the mountains and kindly brought her home. Will you invite him to dine with us? I will be back after I take Adele to her room."

Jean Durand, a tall, wide-shouldered man with arms as strong as tree trunks, relaxed his clenched fists. His large mustache twitched as he approached the younger man, whom he still eyed suspiciously, and shook his hand.

"*Merci, Monsieur Badeau,* for helping my daughter return home. Louis, get some water for monsieur's dog outside, will you?" he said, turning to his son, who stood behind him, staring at the unexpected guest.

Louis went to get the water and returned quickly, standing with his back against the wall, eager to listen to the conversation.

"You must stay and dine with us, Monsieur Badeau," said Jean Durand, following his wife's instructions, although he wasn't quite convinced this strange man was someone he wanted to dine with. He had the air of someone a bit too educated for his liking. Something about him felt a little distant, even arrogant.

"Thank you for the kind invitation, Monsieur Durand, but I have to walk back to Gex," said Jules Badeau.

Now Jean Durand liked this man a little more. Not wanting to walk all the way to Gex late at night was something he could relate to. At least this man did not have a driver with a carriage waiting outside for him, only a scruffy-looking dog.

"Then you must come back another day," he said. "Perhaps next week? On the Sunday after midday, then will you dine with us?"

Monsieur Badeau hesitated for a moment or two. Then he made up his mind.

"With pleasure," replied the schoolteacher. "I shall be delighted to dine with you then. But now I must go."

He put his thick coat back on and shook Jean Durand's hand,

and then the hand of Monsieur Montague, the neighbor who watched this whole scene silently. Jules Badeau walked towards young Louis and made a point of shaking his hand, too.

"*Bonsoir et au revoir,* young man," he said. "See you on Sunday," he added before walking out the door.

Three

I left the hypnotherapist's practice feeling lighter than I did when I walked in, although on some level, I had many more questions that intrigued me. But these questions didn't seem to weigh me down, they sort of uplifted me instead.

I didn't understand why I'd witnessed this strange scene. The experience I'd had was very different from anything I'd expected, or anything I'd experienced before. I thought the hypnotherapist would do some mumbo-jumbo to relieve me of my anxieties and to help me sleep better at night. I did not expect to go into a dreamlike state and see a strange sort of movie in my mind's eye.

Now back on the street, people's faces looked friendlier than they did before, or perhaps for a very long time I just hadn't taken a close look at people passing me on the street. It was as if I'd come out of a shower that washed away many of the stagnant emotions that I'd been suffering from over the past months.

None of it made sense to me, and yet it suddenly all made sense. Why was I even letting myself sink into this self-absorbed depression? *Look at the world, it's beautiful. Look at all these colors, they are so bright.*

"What was that all about?" I asked Tatiana, the therapist, as she brought me back from a faraway journey that – as far as I could tell – had nothing to do with my own life.

She smiled, then shrugged. "I cannot tell you what you went through because you are the one who experienced it fully. I was only your guide, helping you get to something that your subconscious brought up."

"What, was it like a past life or something? I mean, it felt as if it was me, but…it wasn't really… I really don't know what to make of it. It is very confusing."

"Jung spoke of 'collective consciousness', maybe like a download from the Internet where you can get some kind of information that is relevant to you. It isn't necessarily your own experience, but if it helps you understand things, then that's great, right? Or who knows, maybe it was a past-life experience after all. Only you can decide what you believe in, or don't believe in. As I said, I am only the guide into your own subconscious mind. I am only the facilitator."

"Yes, except...I don't understand...who is this Adele? And why is she relevant in my life? Why would my subconscious bring something like this up? Or maybe it was just my imagination?"

"You know," she said, "more often than not the answers come later. Maybe later today, or this week, or in a dream. Or in a future session. Stay with the experience and see if it will make sense to you in the future."

She gave me a recording of the session along with her business card, and told me to wait a week or two before listening to the CD.

"Let things sink in first," she said. "And do write me an email if you have any burning questions that come up."

I started crossing the street, my head full of thoughts about Adele, about her family and about the schoolteacher, about how she let her emotions take over and nearly froze to death because of it. Then the other thoughts came, about how I would now become a much more positive person, how this newfound lightness would in fact serve to create a new 'me', someone who would deal with life in a much more positive way. I was so engrossed in my own thoughts as I crossed the street that I did not notice the small green car turning the corner, and by the time the screeching wail hit my ears and I jumped back to avoid an encounter with the shimmering metal that would surely not be in my favor, the driver managed to hit the brakes.

I kind of expected him to open his window and start shouting at me, telling me that I should be looking before crossing, telling me I was an idiot, a stupid cow, a mindless creature. At least, that's what Don would have done. But this guy didn't. He just sat behind the wheel, frozen, his eyes not really meeting mine, but staring through me above the plastic of the dashboard and the dark green of the front hood.

"Are you ok?" he mouthed, and I nodded. I noticed that he didn't really make eye contact with me, and thought it was strange. It was as if he was looking above my head, not right at me.

Now I was expecting him to step out of the car, to check that I was really all right, but he didn't do that either. He seemed to be as numb as I was, and I just waved a desultory little wave and continued walking. I don't know why I didn't stop to shout at him, tell him he was driving too fast, that he was an idiot. I just walked on, in a daze, as if it didn't matter. And he sat there in the car for a few long moments and then drove on, slowly, carefully, probably blaming himself as much as I blamed myself for not paying enough attention. Relieved that nothing worse had happened.

But there was something that nagged at me, and by the time he was out of sight it was too late to double-check the feeling that just dawned on me – *Hey, I've definitely seen this man before.* But I could not remember where.

And that night, I dreamt of Adele.

Four

She felt as if the week would never end. The first two days of it she was allowed to spend in bed, getting over her fever and bad cold, reading the second volume of Marin le Roy de Gomberville's *Polexandre*. She'd asked for the third volume as her eighteenth birthday present, only two months away. She knew that her parents would make a great effort to purchase it, despite the fact they did not understand her fascination with heroic romance, or with any kind of book for that matter.

"So what is this book about?" asked her mother as Adele desperately tried to finish another page.

"It's wonderful, *Maman*. It is about a man who visits all the sea-coasts, looking for his *amourouse*, Alcidiane. She is a princess and he is…"

"Adele, you have such fanciful ideas. What will become of you? These are just stories, my girl. Life is not like that."

"I know, *Maman*, but I still enjoy reading it. When I read this story I am inside it, it is like I am there, visiting all these wonderful places. And maybe one day I will indeed visit them!"

Her mother sighed, and touched her lips to her daughter's forehead.

"Your fever is gone, Adele. You are lucky that it has not ended in more than just two days in bed. You could have been really sick. Or you could have died, had that man not found you."

"Yes, *Maman*, I know, I am sorry. But he did find me, you see. Things don't always end badly!"

"But they don't always end happily, either. You cannot always count on being lucky or saved by a man. You have to use your head as well, Adele. You are a smart girl. A smart woman. You will be eighteen soon. You need to think about your future."

"Yes, *Maman*, my future. I will write, perhaps, a book like this one. I will visit Paris and London and maybe other places..."

"Adele. Listen to me. I know you dream of all these things, but these are dreams. Your reality might be different. You will perhaps get married, have children..."

"*Maman*, stop it. I am not even eighteen, and I certainly do not plan to get married anytime soon. Perhaps if I travel to Paris, I will meet my future husband there! Perhaps he will be a scholar, or an artist, or even a writer..."

"Adele, scholars and artists and writers cannot necessarily support the lifestyle that you dream of. Neither can school-teachers."

Adele opened her eyes wide, as if horrified. She felt her mouth turning dry.

"Why do you say that, *Maman*?"

"Because it is true. And because your father has invited Monsieur Badeau to dine with us on the Sunday, and we need to plan the meal and to prepare. But..."

Adele waited for her mother to finish the sentence, but her mother hesitated.

"But what, *Maman*?"

"Be careful not to encourage him, Adele. I saw the way he looked at you. You are a pretty girl, a clever young woman. Think of your future."

"Oh, *Maman*! I have no idea what you are talking about. Why would he even look at me? I only met him once, I don't even remember what he looks like..."

Her mother's piercing green eyes met Adele's own blue-gray ones. The mother and daughter stared at each other in silence for a few moments.

"Just remember what I said, Adele," said Anne Durand as she passed her finger over a speckle of dust on her daughter's dressing table. She then got up and left the room, closing the door behind her.

Five

It was Saturday late afternoon and Tom and Jen made dinner – salad and pasta – and the three of us sat around the table together for the first time in weeks. I really appreciated the effort they'd made to try and cheer me up, to spend some time with me. It was the first time they ever made dinner without me asking them to, which probably meant they were truly worried about me.

Life was hectic for them – being a teenager wasn't easy, I could still remember it from twenty-something years back. But they tried their best to keep it together in the difficult weeks following my separation from Don. From careless, selfish teenagers, they seemed to have, at least temporarily, turned into gentle and caring young adults.

"You should get out more, Mom," said Jen while serving herself a large helping of salad. She was in her fourteenth year now, only two years younger than Tom, but much more mature. She had recently started worrying about her looks, whether she was overweight (which she wasn't) or pretty enough (which she was). Both kids had Don's impressive height and his dark, bushy eyebrows. But thankfully, they did not inherit his cynical, often even hurtful, personality. I was hoping they would not develop it later in life.

"I am," I said. "I will. It's just that I brought a lot of work home, and maybe I can even get back to working on my novel…"

"I've been hearing about this novel for years," said Tom, chewing a mouthful of pasta. He was not worried about his weight, and rightfully so. He'd inherited not only Don's impressive height and bushy eyebrows, but also his broad shoulders and athletic physique. The girls were already standing in line for him.

Jen kicked her brother under the table.

"What?" he said.

"Whatever makes Mom happy, Tom," she said. "If she wants to stay in and get on with her novel, that's fine. You know, J.K. Rowling was also like that, nobody knew who she was before she wrote Harry Potter. And she was a single mom," she added.

Tom shrugged.

"Whatever," he said.

We ate in silence and I felt as if I needed to say something, to keep the conversation going.

"I've been to see a hypnotherapist," I said. That got their attention.

"A what?"

Tom stopped eating and stared at me as if I was some strange creature, not his silly old mom.

"A hypnotherapist," I repeated. "It's someone who hypnotizes you, so you can work on different issues in your life. So you can connect with your subconscious."

"You're not losing it, Mom, are you?" he asked and then grunted in pain when Jen kicked him under the table again.

"Ok, whatever," he said again.

"It was actually very interesting," I said, and told them about what I'd experienced, the dreamlike quality of what I saw and felt under hypnosis.

"It was like being nearly asleep, but being aware of things that are going on around me at the same time," I said. "But the dream part was more important to me, as if I chose to focus on it and not on the room I was in, although I knew I was not really inside the dream. Hard to explain, really."

"Sounds awesome," said Jen. "Maybe I should try it, too. I heard that hypnotherapy could also help you lose weight."

The phone rang, and Tom jumped to pick it up. I don't know why he bothered, as his various girlfriends were always messaging him on Facebook and WhatsApp and would probably not call his home number. In fact, people rarely called our home number these days, as we all had mobile phones.

"Yeah, she's here," I heard him say. "Yes, hold on."

"For you, Mom," he shouted from the other room and I got up to take the call. *Must be someone from the office,* I remember thinking. *Although why would they call my home number, on a Saturday night? What can be so urgent?*

But the voice on the other side was not a familiar one.

"Hi, Amelia? This is…this is Noah here. Noah Welder."

There was a moment of silence while I searched my memory files. The name kind of rang a bell…but a very small and distant one. Yes, I'd definitely heard it before. Was it one of the authors from the past? No one I had worked with recently, that's for sure.

"I am sorry, do we know each other?" I finally asked.

"I almost ran you over yesterday," he said.

"Oh," was all that I could say. Of course I remembered the incident, but how the hell did this man get my number?

"We also went to school together," he said. "I was the shy geek in tenth grade at Abraham Lincoln's in San Francisco. I don't think you spoke more than a few words to me back then."

"Oh," I said again. "I am so sorry, but I really don't remember…."

"In the summer of 1985 when you moved to New York, you said that you'd come back to visit often. Do you go back to the Bay Area regularly?"

I didn't know what to say. Was this guy for real? I did vaguely remember a few geeky boys in my San Francisco high school, but that was such a long time ago. It was just a few years after I'd moved to the US from Paris, where I was born to expatriate American parents, and the whole American experience was not completely new but quite overwhelming. Those first few years were floating in a hazy cloud of memory, especially as that was when I also discovered makeup, boys and recreational drugs. How did he remember me? How did he even recognize me?

"But of course." He interrupted my train of thought. "I remember seeing you back in San Francisco in 1989, I think it was July, wasn't it? We bumped into each other on the street and you said you came back to visit a friend."

I didn't know what to say. Was this some kind of joke? But it was true. I was back in San Francisco and spent a week at my friend Rebecca's. Maybe it was in 1989, I had no idea; that was so long ago now.

"Yes... I was back and stayed with a friend, maybe it was 1989, I don't know...how do you remember that? I hardly remember anything from back then."

He laughed, the phone line echoing his laughter in my ear. I got goose bumps, this was getting a bit too much for me. I considered hanging up.

"My mind works in strange ways." He then said quietly, "It's related to my condition. Anyway, I figured I'd try and find you and apologize for nearly running you over yesterday. It took me a moment or two to recognize you, although you haven't changed much. You're just as beautiful."

"I am sure I have," I said. "But I appreciate the compliment."

And then I asked what was really on my mind. "I do remember you nearly running me over yesterday, but...how did you find me? My home number?"

"I just googled you," he said. "The Internet rewards the curious."

I wasn't sure I liked where this seemed to be going.

"Well, anyway, I just wanted to say I was sorry for nearly running you over," he repeated.

"That's ok," I said. "You didn't."

"I'm sure glad about that," he said. "Have a nice evening."

"You too," I said, but it was too late, as he'd already hung up.

Creepy, I thought. And then I saw that Jen and Tom had gone to their rooms, only partially clearing the dinner table. I reluctantly finished the job, stuffed the dirty dishes into the dishwasher, turned it on, made myself a cup of coffee and sat at my computer. Hesitantly, I opened the novel file, which had not been updated for months now. And I started typing.

Six

Adele awoke on Sunday morning as soon as the first rays of sun hit her windowsill. She stretched her arms over her head and stayed under the covers for a while, contemplating the day ahead.

Her mother's words rang in her ears. *Scholars and artists and writers cannot necessarily support the lifestyle that you dream of. Neither can schoolteachers,* said her mother. And she was probably right. But was the idea of her, Adele, supporting herself through her own work, rather than having to count on a man to support her, so ridiculous, she wondered. Perhaps it was, but she did not want to find herself with a man she didn't care for just because he was a good provider. Unless, she thought, unless that man was an adventurer, someone who could take her to see all those places she wanted so badly to visit. But someone like that could surely not be found in her village, not even in the nearby town. To meet a man like that she would need to go to the city, to Lyon, maybe even to Paris. Yes, Paris, that was where all the exciting things happened and the adventurous roamed freely.

She got out of bed and sat at her dressing table. Picking up her large horsehair brush, she started brushing her hair, counting the strokes. One, two, three…she stopped at forty. She then started untangling her long, wavy hair with a comb, but then decided that was more than enough. For after all, and despite the excitement she admitted to feeling in the pit of her stomach about the special guest coming later that day, didn't her mother say that she should not encourage him? And besides, she didn't know anything about him. Perhaps he was already married?

She tied her hair back, washed and dressed and made her way to the kitchen, where her mother supervised the chopping of vegetables into small pieces for ratatouille, a vegetable stew. Marie, the young woman who'd come and help at their household together with her little sister every time they had guests, had already been to the market in Gex and bought a small turkey, which she was now preparing for frying with bread-crumbs and serving with ravigote sauce.

Anne Durand handed her daughter a cloth and instructed her to polish the porcelain plates and the silverware they kept for special occasions. Adele could not help but wonder why her mother was going to all this trouble if she didn't want to encourage the schoolteacher. Was it because he was an educated man, and she didn't want to give the impression of being a family of peasants? After all, her mother did come from a better background than her father, but all she had to prove for it now was this set of porcelain crockery.

Adele ran her finger over the blue flower pattern on the shiny white porcelain, and images of a grand dining-room immediately rushed to her mind.

"*Maman*, tell me again where we got these plates?" she asked.

Her mother sighed. "They were a wedding gift for your father and me," she said, wiping her hands on her apron. "I've told you this before. It was the best wedding gift we got, this and the silverware you are going to polish, if you ever stop asking questions and start working."

Adele knew her mother was a hardworking woman who expected of herself at least what she expected of others, so did not let her mother's harsh words offend her. But she did dare ask one more question, because she really wanted to know. "Is there anyone else coming to eat with us, or is it just...just Monsieur Badeau?"

Perhaps the presence of a more important guest could explain the feverish preparations, she thought.

Anne Durand stared at her daughter, her eyes narrow and inquisitive. "Who else would you want to invite, Adele?" she asked quietly.

"*Non, Maman,* it is just that it has been so long since the last time you took these plates out and I thought that maybe it was someone important…"

"Don't be ungrateful, Adele. Monsieur Badeau saved your life. He is important. This, of course, does not mean that you should—" She stopped in mid-sentence as she noticed Marie and her little sister watching them, drinking in their every word. She had no doubt that these two would later repeat everything they heard and saw in the Durand household.

"Back to work, you two!" she commanded. "Some things don't concern you," she added and turned to face her daughter again.

"You too, Adele, we don't have all day. If you cannot do your work quietly in the kitchen perhaps you should take these plates and silverware and go and set the table."

Adele looked at her fingertips, embarrassed by the fact her mother had scolded her in front of Marie. She carefully picked up the five precious porcelain plates and carried them to the dining-room, where an ironed, white tablecloth had already been spread on the dining-table.

She carefully wiped the plates, one by one, and placed them in front of each chair. At their side she laid the polished silverware. Who would sit where? she wondered. Her father would sit at the head of the table, of course. Then perhaps she would sit next to her brother on one side of the table, and her mother would sit next to Monsieur Badeau. But would he sit across from her? Or across from her brother?

Glancing behind her to make sure no one was looking, she went to the chair where she thought perhaps Monsieur Badeau would sit, and ran her fingers across the back. The grained wood felt slick under her fingers, and she imagined Jules Badeau leaning on it. A shiver went down her spine. What was she doing? How silly of her.

She took a clean cloth and wiped the back of the chairs from invisible dust – all six chairs. She then decided to take one chair away. There was no point in having a chair without a plate in front of it, was there? And besides, this would increase the chance of Monsieur Badeau sitting right across from her, she thought. She took the extra chair and put it at the corner of the dining room, near the tall wooden cupboard, rearranging the plates and silverware so close to the empty edge of the table that sitting there would become awkward without moving all the plates closer together.

"Can I use the special glasses, *Maman*?" she called towards the kitchen.

"Yes, but be careful when you take them out of the cupboard," her mother called back.

Adele turned the large key and opened the cupboard door. Two rows of crystal glasses stood there, shining in a splendor, which transported Adele straight back to the images of Parisian balls she entertained in her mind so often. She gently touched the stems of the beautiful glasses, counting all twelve of them. She then took out five glasses one by one, wiping them with the edge of her apron before setting them in front of each plate.

She admired her own work, moving the plates and silverware just a little closer to the empty edge of the table, before turning the key and locking the cupboard again.

"There we go," she said out loud. "All done, *Maman*."

Seven

No, no, no. I would not accept this kind of writing from my authors. As an editor, I didn't appreciate that the entire scene was around the setting of the dinner-table. Nothing actually *happened*, it was all in Adele's head. No, this wasn't good writing. It was slow-paced and the scene did not really serve to advance the story – but something stopped me from hitting the delete key and getting rid of the scene on the screen in front of me. Maybe it was the fact that the scene practically wrote itself, after months of my not being able to write anything new. Where did this story come from? Did this really emerge from my own subconscious?

I looked at the top-right corner of my screen – it was nearly midnight. Where did time go? Jen had gone for a sleepover at Tammy's house – her best friend living just three streets away. She'd asked me several times whether I'd be ok. Of course I would be ok, I reassured her. I had work to finish. In fact, it was Jen that I was worried about. I was happy for her to go and spend time with her friend. She'd been a little moody lately, not her usual cheerful self.

Something'd been going on in her mind, but I couldn't figure out what. I hoped it was just raging teenage hormones.

Talking of raging teenage hormones, Tom was in his room, his door closed. I could hear the beat of the rap music so I knew he was not asleep. He was probably chatting to his friends online.

I felt strangely alert after having spent three hours in front of my computer, typing away. Although it was a Saturday night and I knew I could sleep in the next morning, I pretty much forced myself to go to bed. I was not tired, but I knew I needed the sleep.

But all alone in the big bed, the soft sheets caressing my skin,

I could not fall asleep. As hard as I tried, sleep seemed to escape me; and drifting between there and wakefulness, more images started coming before my closed eyes.

Eight

Jules Badeau waved – a small controlled gesture – as he walked away from the Durand house. Adele waved back and stood in silence next to her brother Louis, worried that he would hear her heart pounding. She wondered why Monsieur Badeau preferred to walk back home to Gex, instead of arranging for a carriage to pick him up. Perhaps he liked walking. Or perhaps he could not afford the carriage.

Louis looked her in the eye, for they were exactly the same height although she was three years older than him.

"What?" she said.

"Nothing," he answered and then poked her in the ribs, making her jolt.

"Stop your nonsense," she cried out, and was horrified when she saw Monsieur Badeau's head turn towards them in the distance. He must have heard her. How unwomanly of her.

"Only if you stop yours," said Louis. "I'd say you like this man."

"He's all right," said Adele, her cheeks blushing as she struggled to even the tone of her voice.

Her right hand, the one Jules Badeau touched earlier, felt as if it was on fire. She could still feel his fingers where they had hardly touched her palm as he said goodbye.

Why is this? she wondered. *He is not a strikingly handsome man. He is not an impressive man until you get to know him. But once you do, the energy coming from him is like that of a water cascade, or a majestic mountain on a spring day, or a...*

"Adele!"

Her mother's voice shook her from her daydream and she noticed that Louis was nowhere to be seen. Probably gone wandering off again, for it was fine for him to go and play in the fields. She was expected to help clean up.

"Yes, *Maman*, I am coming," she called, and walked back into the house, where her mother was supervising Marie and her little sister who were washing up the precious, festive plates. She, Adele, was no washing girl. She deserved better than cleaning up after guests and worrying about such unimportant matters. All she really wanted now was to be left in peace to wander around the house in this daze that she enjoyed so much, so very much. She wanted to have some time for herself, some time to think.

And yet, she helped her mother fold away the tablecloth, which in some amazing stroke of luck remained unstained – perhaps because the schoolteacher did not drink wine and her father did not want to make a bad impression with his habitual Sunday drinking. Not that her father didn't drink at all, of course he did – he just managed to pour it all straight down his throat this time, and none of it on the white tablecloth.

Why didn't the schoolteacher drink? she wondered. Was it that he wanted to keep a certain façade? Or perhaps he just did not like the taste of wine? The concept that a grown man would refuse a glass of wine at lunchtime was foreign to her. It made the schoolteacher even more mysterious, more intriguing.

She started gathering the cloth napkins when she noticed her mother staring at her.

"What, *Maman*?"

"What did you think?"

"Of what, *Maman*?"

"Of him, of course. Don't try to fool me, girl. I might not read as many books as you do, but you know very well I am not stupid."

"*Maman*, of course not…I…I just don't know what to say."

"How about you speak the truth? That would be a good start."

"Yes, the truth. I like him, *Maman*, but I don't know much about him. He is not a strikingly handsome man, and I know he is not well off…but there is something about him…something strong and kind…he is so smart, and has a good heart."

Her mother listened in silence, and then nodded in agreement.

"That is exactly what worries me, Adele. I like him, too. He is a good, kind man. But I think perhaps you need more than that. You need someone who will give you a good life, the kind of life that will allow you to…" She hesitated.

Adele knew what her mother wanted to say, and yet she wanted her to say it in her own words. For she, Adele, had never expressed much enthusiasm about any of the young men who courted her, who sent their mothers and fathers to speak to her parents. Not even about Pierre Bertrand, who threw hints her way every time they visited his family's shop in Gex, although she did like his stylish clothes and the knowledgeable way he spoke about the latest trends in Paris and London. He had even visited Paris – twice. He once said that he would take her there one day and she laughed because she thought that he meant it as a joke. Her mother scolded her later, for being so impolite.

The Bertrands were a family of merchants who not only travelled extensively to the port towns of Nantes, Bordeaux and La Rochelle, but were always dressed in the finest clothes and had a big house right in the center of town, not far from the church. Adele's mother mentioned to her father, when she thought Adele was not listening, that Pierre, the second son of the three Bertrand boys, would make an excellent husband for Adele. The older Bertrand boy was already married, and the youngest one, Adele's age, was a quiet and simple young man. *Too quiet and not clever enough for Adele. But Pierre Bertrand, he would make a good husband, and it is obvious that he likes Adele,* said Anne Durand. Jean Durand grunted in response to his wife's observations.

Now Adele's mother seemed lost for words. She just shook her head and walked towards the kitchen with the folded tablecloth in her hands.

"Here you go, Marie. There are no wine stains but take it and wash it nonetheless. Who knows, we might need it again soon."

This was their one fine tablecloth, and it was only used once or twice a year. The rest of the time they dined on a simple table-cloth, which had a few wine and grease stains that never came off despite fervent scrubbing by both Marie and Madame Durand, who thought that perhaps Marie was just being lazy and didn't try hard enough to remove the stains.

Sometimes they used no tablecloth at all, like many of their farmer neighbors – for what was the point of getting a fine table-cloth dirty when the wooden table could be just wiped clean?

"C'est pour le plaisir," explained Anne to her husband Jean, who posed this very question more than once. "It is for the pleasure – of the eyes and of the heart."

He just shrugged this answer off and bent his head down to his spoon.

"The pleasures of the eyes and of the heart are women's business," he said after he wiped his bowl clean with a thick chunk of bread, torn with his fingers from the half-loaf that sat in front of his plate. "I just want a full stomach".

"At the Bertrand household, they dine on fine linen every single day," said their neighbor, Madame Montague, when she came over for tea one afternoon. "And not only do they dine on fine linen every single day, they also have oranges on the table on weekdays and Madame Bertrand was seen wearing a hat made of Canadian beaver-skin last winter. Can you imagine, wearing a hat made from an animal coming all the way from Canada?"

Madame Montague said the last sentence as if it was the most glorious of all dreams, to wear a hat made of some poor rodent's skin.

Adele would have been happy with something more modest, such as a blue-gray silk dress, and the silk did not have to come from far away. She'd be perfectly happy with European silk, as long as the color matched her eyes.

But for a couple of hours, when she sat right across from the man who had come to dine with them earlier that day, she did not care about the clothes he was wearing. Her cunning plan had worked and her mother sat Monsieur Badeau between herself and her husband, and instructed Adele's brother to sit across from her, leaving Adele the place across from the guest. Adele was pleased that she could now examine him without having to glance sideways, and she did notice his handsome wool jacket – probably his Sunday best – and a smart white *cravat* that made his long eyelashes and wavy dark hair stand out, even though the *cravat* was somewhat outdated.

"In Paris," said Madame Montague on another of her afternoon visits, "no one wears *cravats* anymore. Everyone now wears stocks with a black *solitaire*. Now that," she concluded, "is a refined style."

But Jules Badeau did not seem to care much about the latest fashions in Paris as a topic of conversation, and he spent the afternoon discussing political reforms with her father, who said – after drinking two glasses of wine – that the king was not only fat and ten times worse than a lowly thief but was also a selfish coward. Adele waited to hear Monsieur Badeau's response to her father's profound observations but he only nodded with a half-smile, as if to say: *I agree with you, Monsieur Durand, but you'll have to get me to drink at least two glasses of wine before I'll admit to it.*

The only thing he did say in reply to her father's comments was that he found it strange that Monsieur Durand chose to name his only son after a king he disliked so much, and that made everyone around the table laugh. They could even hear Marie laughing in the kitchen, which confirmed what Adele and her mother always suspected – that instead of working she listened in to the conversations in their household.

As for Adele, she thought that although her father had a point when he described King Louis XV thus, if he wanted a safe place to keep his wool cap on for a few more decades, he should drink less and mind his own business more.

Of course, she did not dare to voice this opinion as she was not even eighteen yet and knew that, under the close watch her mother kept on her every single second from diagonally across the table, she would not get away with speaking her mind this time without an embarrassing scolding that would surely follow. And she certainly did not want to be treated like a child and sent to her room in the presence of Jules Badeau.

And as for the king's namesake on Adele's right, he looked completely bored with the conversation going on around the lunch table and she had to step on his toes three times to stop him picking his nose.

Now that the meal was over and Monsieur Badeau headed back to his humble home in Gex – Adele knew nothing of his home of course, but she tried very hard to imagine it – she found herself wishing he were still there with them. Perhaps he lacked glamour and did not adhere to the latest styles of Paris, but he could certainly hold an interesting conversation and had a great sense of humor.

She felt as if he had not only saved her life once, but possibly twice. The first time was on that horrible cold day just over a week before, when she got so stupidly lost in the mountains. The second time might be by introducing some interest into her life, because otherwise, even though she was probably smart enough not to get lost in the mountains again and freeze to death, there was a most definite risk that if her life continued exactly as it was before she'd met him, she would die of boredom.

Nine

I could hardly believe my eyes when I looked at the small alarm clock on my nightstand. It showed 11 a.m., which must have meant I'd slept for at least…ten hours. I honestly couldn't remember the last time this had happened – years ago, surely. So maybe this hypnotherapy thing was doing something, after all. Then I remembered the images I had seen just before I fell asleep, but I couldn't hold on to the details, they had a dreamlike quality to them, although I was sure I didn't dream them. There was Adele, and that schoolteacher again, having dinner with her family…it all faded away now. I was awake, awake enough to remember that there was something, somewhere in my mind, something swirling like a stain of ink in a glass of clear water, and I could not quite hold on to it.

As I made my first coffee of the day – I had tried hard to cut down as I thought it might help my sleep patterns, but I could not forego my morning coffee – the phone rang.

What's up with this? It was too early to be one of the kids' friends – they probably didn't wake up before midday – and I couldn't think of anyone who'd call me on a Sunday morning, even if it was almost noon by now. But then, I immediately recognized the voice at the other end of the line.

"Hi, Amelia…"

"Oh, hi."

Not him again, I thought. *What does he want? He really creeps me out.*

"You've recognized my voice."

"Well, yes," I said. "We only spoke a few hours ago."

"So sorry to disturb you, I was just wondering… I was wondering if you'd like to meet for coffee this afternoon? I mean,

I know we haven't seen each other in over twenty years and you probably don't even know who I am but I thought that maybe this chance encounter the other day..."

He paused.

"Yes?"

"Anyway, sorry if I've disturbed you, you're probably doing things with your family on Sunday and this was a very silly idea anyway, I just thought..."

Something in me suddenly felt sorry for him. He was probably still a geeky man, and if I was horrible to him in high school, which I honestly could not remember, maybe I could somehow be nice to him now, just for an hour or so, and make up for it. Lauren was always talking about karma – who knew, maybe karma was real? Besides, I was now curious. I'd lost touch with the vast majority of my high-school friends since moving to New York. Maybe he could tell me something about where people were, what they were doing now.

Why not, I then thought. I didn't have any other plans for the day, and the kids had their own plans. They would certainly not mind if I went out.

"Ok," I said.

"Ok what?"

"Ok, let's meet for coffee."

"Really? That's great... I...I am actually at work now, at the Manhattan Fencing Center, until three so maybe we can meet right after..."

"Give me the address," I said. "I'll meet you there at three."

I wanted to be in control, do the coming and going, decide when I'd had enough if he were really strange. It would also give me a few more hours to write, to try and capture last night's images. I'd try to satisfy my curiosity about this weirdo who emerged from my past and then I'd get on with my afternoon. Maybe even go for a power walk in Central Park, something I'd meant to do for months and somehow hadn't found the time or motivation to do. Coffee was as good a reason as any to get out of the house. I wrote down the address and hung up, then grabbed a yogurt from the fridge and sat by my computer again.

The story flew out of my fingertips and onto the keyboard.

Ten

It was an unusually gray day for the month of June, although misty days were not uncommon at the foothills of the Jura even in the summer months. The clouds sat on the mountain range like a cap covering a bald scalp, preventing the cold from making it uncomfortable but also keeping the warm sunshine away.

"We will take a carriage to Gex tomorrow morning," Madame Durand had said the previous day, "and buy some fabric for a new dress for you, Adele."

"Oh, *Maman*, thank you," she said, imagining a flowing gown of pale color that would catch the blue hues in her otherwise gray eyes.

"Well, you'll be turning eighteen next month, and you need a new dress to celebrate, don't you," said her mother matter-of-factly.

They were not underprivileged, but new clothes were certainly not an everyday thing. In fact, Adele had six different dresses, which was far more than any of the girls she knew in the village owned. Four of the dresses were practical, everyday ones, and the two good dresses were now almost worn out and certainly too short. She had hoped she would get a new dress for her eighteenth birthday, but she wouldn't have dared ask for one had her mother not offered.

"Monsieur Garnier will come to get us, so we can be in Gex mid-morning," said her mother.

Adele was up early to make sure she had plenty of time to wash, dress and braid her hair. Gex was a small town and wasn't very far away, but it was certainly a treat to go out there, see all the people, hear the latest gossip. She chose one of her two special dresses, the one which was a bit too small at the underarms, and ran her fingers on the delicate embroidery on the sleeves. She had inherited this green dress from her cousin, Marie-Elise, who was slightly smaller in build than herself and when she married a neighboring farmer's son at the age of twenty, she gave away her old clothes and exchanged them for matronly, practical dresses, as if saying that there was no hope she would need beautiful clothes ever again.

Shortly after she got the dress from Marie-Elise, Adele understood why her cousin gave her dresses away so quickly – she simply could not fit into them anymore, and needed larger, more flowing gowns to accommodate her growing belly. *A child at the age of twenty is surely the end of life,* thought Adele, but didn't dare voice this opinion. She wanted children of her own, of course, some day. But not before she was much, much older. Twenty-three, twenty-four, maybe even as old as twenty-six! She wanted to visit many wonderful places and do interesting things, like those people she read about in her novels. She could not understand everything she read but she loved those books nonetheless – everything about them – the way they looked, felt and smelled. And she was the proud owner of three books. She didn't know anyone her age that had three books. Not even her brother Louis.

"Are you ready, Adele? I will help you with the corset!"

Her mother's voice brought her back to her room, where the gray skies covered the view of the majestic mountains that she could see from her window on clear days.

Anne Durand was watching her from the doorway.

"*Oui, Maman,* thank you," she said and turned her back to her mother. "Will we have time to go to visit Madame LeRoy, *Maman*? Please? I would like to choose another book. I am almost finished with the one I am reading and..."

"Breathe in," her mother commanded and Adele took a deep breath. Madame Durand pulled on the strings of her daughter's corset and then tied them together.

"You look very nice today for our trip to Gex, my dear," said her mother. It was a half question, half statement, which made Adele wonder what her mother had in mind.

"*Merci, Maman.*"

"You never know who you might meet in town, right?" said her mother and turned to leave the room. "Put that yellow ribbon in your hair, it makes you look very pretty," she added before she closed the door behind her.

Adele slipped into her dress, and turned around in front of the mirror to examine herself from the back. She combed her hair and tied the yellow ribbon in it, pinched both her cheeks, and when satisfied with her looks headed downstairs to have her breakfast before heading into town. She decided to be on her best behavior, so her mother would agree to take her to Madame LeRoy, who had a small collection of books she was happy to lend to those few young people interested in reading them.

The sun had come out through the clouds by the time they arrived in Gex. The few streets of the small town, just wide enough for a carriage to pass through, looked bright and inviting in the sunshine. Adele stuck her head out of the carriage window and breathed in the air. She was only a short distance away from her home in Chevry, but the air felt different. There was something exciting about being here in Gex, even if it was far from what she imagined Lyon or Paris to be like. She would definitely prefer to live here instead of in the small village where she was born. But a city would be so much better of course, somewhere like Lyon, which was half a day away, or even Paris, but it would take so long to get there; three or four days by carriage.

"Adele, put your head back inside if you don't want it chopped off!" commanded her mother. "Look at you now, your ribbon is all messed up."

"*Oui, Maman,*" said Adele sweetly, remembering her resolution to behave properly so her mother would agree to call at Madame LeRoy's. Adele knew that her mother was a practical woman, and did not see the use of all the books she tried to read. Anne Durand could read, which was not very common for a woman in their parts. *But what use is there in reading all these books?* her mother often asked.

What a waste of time for a woman, Adele heard her say on several occasions. She wouldn't dare say such a thing in the company of Madame LeRoy, who loved to read and was one of the wealthiest women in town. In fact, she was related to the Bertrands, a second cousin of some sort.

But Adele knew that there were so many other things Madame Durand would prefer her daughter did, such as improve her embroidery and sewing, and of course, her cooking skills. But Adele was stubborn, and she made sure her mother knew that. Recently, she felt her mother was beginning to soften towards her, just a little bit. She knew that her mother loved her and wanted the best for her, she just had a funny way of showing it sometimes.

The carriage stopped and the two women gathered their skirts and stepped down into the street.

"Merci, Monsieur Garnier," said her mother. "Please meet us here in about three hours, to take us home."

"Oui, Madame Durand, bien sûr," said the driver and cracked his whip to prompt his horse to gallop off.

Three hours! thought Adele. *This means that there will be time to go and get another book.* But she did not say a thing, for fear her mother would change her mind, although of course now that the driver had taken off she could not easily do so. Adele smiled at her mother, and noticed in the bright sunlight how pretty her face was. *Pretty, but looking much older than she used to,* thought Adele. But she had to stop staring and follow the matronly Anne Durand, who was striding purposefully towards the Bertrand shop. *Will Pierre Bertrand be there?* wondered Adele.

She did not have to wonder for long, because as soon as they approached the shop he hurried to open the door for them, as if he was expecting their arrival.

"*Madame Durand.*" He turned towards her mother first. "Looking beautiful, as always."

"*Bonjour, Pierre,*" replied her mother courteously.

"And Adele." He now turned towards her. "Like mother, like daughter."

"Thank you, Monsieur Bertrand," she answered, teasing him. She knew he would protest.

"Oh, Adele, please don't call me that, it makes me feel as if I am thirty years old. I am only a few years your senior, I don't look that old, do I?"

Adele noticed Pierre was wearing a stock, with a black *solitaire* that was neatly tied around his hair in the back of his head, holding it together in an elegant knot.

"How stylish," she commented, pointing at his stock and Pierre smiled, pleased that she had noticed.

"I got it last month, it is the latest fashion in Paris," he said.

Madame Durand busied herself with the small selection of fabrics at the back of the store, but Adele sensed she was looking at them from the corner of her eye.

"So I heard you had a small misadventure recently," said Pierre.

Adele raised her eyebrows.

"Oh?" she said. Rumors travelled fast in these parts.

"You could not find your way home, apparently," he continued.

She felt her cheeks getting hot.

"How do you know that?"

"Oh, *ma belle*, this is a small town."

"Did...did Monsieur Badeau...did he tell everyone? How unkind of him!"

Pierre Bertrand smiled. "Do not worry, *ma belle*, it is not your gallant savior who told the entire town, but the lovely Madame

Montague who visited here a few days ago. You know how she loves to talk."

"How about this one, Adele?"

Her mother interrupted the conversation, waving towards a roll of mustard-yellow fabric.

"It is pretty, *Maman*, but..."

Adele approached the rolls of fabric in the back of the store and stood in front of them, running her fingers across two or three rolls before she noticed a blue-gray one, placed a short distance from all the other fabrics. It looked exquisite, of a much better quality than all the other cloths. Adele ran her fingers on the blue-gray fabric, and found it hard to pull them away.

"How about this one, *Maman*?"

"This has just arrived from Paris, Madame Durand," said Pierre Bertrand, who now stood behind Adele's mother. "Your daughter has very good taste. Of course, it is more expensive than the other fabrics, which is why we've put it separately, but it is of a much better quality."

Anne Durand hesitated for a moment, considering her words.

"This is much too old for you, Adele," she finally exclaimed. "You are turning eighteen, not thirty."

"*Maman*, but look how pretty it is, how delicate...how..."

"It is very sophisticated, Madame Durand," intervened Pierre. "It just arrived last month from Paris," he repeated, as if he thought this would convince Anne Durand of the superiority of the fabric. "It arrived the same time as this." He pointed to his own frilly white stock.

Adele smiled at him with gratitude for intervening in her favor.

"You see, *Maman*, it just arrived from Paris. It is so fashionable and so..."

"Where would you even wear something like this around here?" her mother interrupted. "It is not practical, Adele."

Adele touched the silky cloth. "*Oui, Maman*, but I have

stopped growing now and this would be good for many years and maybe one day I will be invited somewhere nice and could wear it."

Pierre hesitantly raised his hand. "I don't wish to contradict you, *madame*, but your daughter would look fabulous in this, and it will bring out her beautiful eyes. And it would make for a perfect dress for a journey to Paris, for example. Of course, I can give you a special price for it," he added when he noticed Anne Durand was still hesitating.

Madame Durand laughed, but it was not a joyous laughter.

"This silly girl and her dreams about Paris. Who will take you to Paris, Adele? Don't be unreasonable."

Pierre Bertrand cleared his throat.

"I have no doubt, *madame*, that many young men would be honored to take your daughter to Paris."

Madame Durand laughed again. This time the bitterness was gone from her laughter, and it sounded lighter, almost mocking.

"Who, Pierre, the local peasants?" she uttered the last two words as if she had a bad taste in her mouth.

"*Maman!*"

Adele could not believe her mother's directness. And her mother scolded her for being impolite!

Pierre Bertrand shifted his weight from one leg to another. "I, for one, *madame*, would be honored if a woman such as your daughter would consider..."

"Don't be silly, Pierre," interrupted Madame Durand. "Your family would never agree to this."

There was an awkward silence and Adele felt tears stinging her eyes. What was her mother thinking? How could she talk about her own daughter as if she was some kind of faulty produce, a rotten potato or a worm-ridden apple?

"We will take the yellow fabric, Pierre," said Madame Durand. "A husband who can take my Adele to Paris would surely be able to buy her fabric for a new dress. Now we need to be practical and get fabric for a dress she can wear on her eighteenth birthday, and the party will be in Madame Montague's barn, not in Paris. You are cordially invited, by the way."

Adele's heart sank as she watched Pierre Bertrand cut three *toises* of the mustardy-yellow fabric, fold it into a neat square and hand it to her mother. The yellow was pretty but so...so childish. The blue-gray fabric was exactly what she wanted, it was so luxurious and so...how did Pierre Bertrand call it? So *sophisticated*.

"What is this sad face, girl? Don't be ungrateful!" her mother scolded her after they said their goodbyes to Pierre Bertrand and left the store.

"*Non, Maman*, I am really happy about this new dress," Adele forced the words out of her mouth. "I look forward to helping you make it."

"Good," said Madame Durand. "Now, let's go see Madame LeRoy for those silly books of yours."

Eleven

I arrived just after three, and as I pushed open the glass door of the Manhattan Fencing Center I felt as if I'd stepped into another universe.

Teenagers dressed in white and sparkly silver lamé jackets strutted down the corridor, ignoring me – the middle-aged woman who stood there, gaping at them as if she'd never seen anything like it before in her entire life. In fact, I hadn't.

When Noah Welder said 'fencing' I initially thought of fences, but of course, then remembered there was a sport by that name – in fact, I even remembered it was an Olympic sport. But I didn't quite expect...this.

These young people clad in bright white outfits, holding their masks in one hand and their weapons in the other, were rushing to change into their Sunday-afternoon clothes, to go and finish their homework or play with their friends. Teens roughly the same age as Jen and Tom seemed so much more mature, determined, glowing, than the two teenagers I had left back home in front of their computers. Jen had made it back from her friend's house just before I left.

"It's awesome that you're going out, Mom," she said before she sat down to have yet another chat on Facebook. "It's such a nice day, shame to have you sitting in front of your computer all day."

I agreed, and didn't point out to her that she was doing just that – sitting in front of her computer on such a beautiful and sunny day.

A man dressed in black walked towards me, and it took me a few seconds to realize that indeed, there was something familiar about him.

"Hi, Amelia," he said and shook my hand. Something was unusual, slightly strange about this man called Noah Welder. I couldn't put my finger on it but he wasn't quite looking me in the eye, it was more as if he was looking through me.

"It's a pleasure to see you again after all this time. Such a coincidence that we are both here after all these years. I didn't think I would ever see you again, despite the fact that when we last saw each other, you said you would keep in touch. I was just leaving my previous workplace – which was not my workplace back then but I spent a lot of time there – when I crossed you on the street, but I am still not sure you actually remembered me."

I needed a break after his monologue. It threw me back for a moment or two.

"I think I actually do now," was all that I could manage to say back to him. Seeing this man now, I vaguely remembered a thin boy, wearing glasses. In front of me was a tall, wide-shouldered man, his black coaching attire adding some confidence to his posture. Could that really be the shy boy I sort of remembered?

"I'll just go and change quickly," he said.

"Sure," I said.

As we walked down 7th Avenue and picked a café on 7th and 40th Street, I got the strangest feeling. It was as if this were some kind of preplanned event. Not by me – and not even by this man walking next to me, who now, after he'd changed into a pair of jeans and a burgundy t-shirt, looked more like the geek I vaguely remembered from twenty-something years back. But it still felt almost as if it were meant to be.

"That's so strange," I said. "I mean, who'd think that someone I knew in San Francisco twenty years back would almost run me over in New York?"

"I had to come all the way here and to almost run you over to have you pay attention to me," he said, his face straight and serious, as he held the café door open for me.

I must have sounded nervous as I laughed. He was surely

joking. Or was he serious?

"How long have you been living here?" I asked, as we sat at a small table.

"Only two years," he said. "Before I moved here I worked at Halberstadt Fencers Club in San Francisco. That's the place I walked out of when we met last time. It's the same club I started at when I was ten, in 1979. A week after my tenth birthday my mother decided I needed to do something that would help me focus, and took me there. Ever since, I've been dedicated to fencing with Aspergerian single-mindedness. Fencing, and of course, chess, which was always my Aspergerian passion."

"Oh," I said. The coin just dropped for me. His openness threw me back, but it also explained some of the oddities I'd noticed. I felt relieved, suddenly able to relax. "So you've become a fencing instructor. Hiding behind a mask to avoid social interactions," I said.

He nodded, still not looking me directly in the eye. "I am the only non-Eastern European fencing instructor at Manhattan Fencing," he said, as if he'd been just awarded a medal. "So I guess I did something right along the way, because these Eastern-European guys are awesome fencers, and instructors."

I suddenly felt compassion for this boy-like man. I just wished I could remember more about him.

"So we went to the same school, right?" I asked. I wanted to get more information, encourage my memory to fish out forgotten details from my distant past.

"Yes, Abraham Lincoln. You were in 10b, I was in 10d, and then you moved to the East Coast the following year," he said. "You were friends with Margery Wilson and Rebecca Wright. You have a brother called Dillon and you lived on 520 Balboa Street. I know, because you once told me."

I felt the hairs on the back of my neck standing.

"How do you remember all these details?" I asked.

He laughed, as if my question was funny. "My mind works in

strange ways," he said. "There's nothing I can do about it. I managed to improve my social skills over the years, but I am still more than happy to hide behind the fencing mask and deal with people individually. It helps me avoid social blunders."

I didn't quite know what to say to that. His directness was somewhat overwhelming, but I also felt respect for this directness – he wasn't trying to pretend.

"So when I googled you I saw you were in publishing," he said.

"It freaks me out that you know all these things about me, and I can hardly remember you," I said before I could stop myself. Something about his raw openness made me forget my own social manners. It was as if he'd opened some kind of primal line of communication that I wasn't aware of previously.

"It's all on the Internet," he said. "I am sorry, I didn't mean to stalk you, just to find you and apologize for nearly running you over. I should have stopped, I guess; I should have made sure you were okay, but I am not very good in this kind of situation. And then I recognized you. It took me a couple of minutes to make the connection and by then you were gone. Or I was gone."

I didn't know what to say to that, so I just nodded.

"You know, the high-school years were the worst years of my life. That's when everyone turned to social-emotional stuff. That's exactly the kind of thing I was not good at, I am still not good at. So I guess this meeting is a little like closing a circle for me. I suppose it was important to me for that reason."

"I understand," I said. "I am sorry if I wasn't nice to you in high school."

I honestly didn't remember if I was or I wasn't.

"It's not that," he said. "It's that I didn't fit in, so life wasn't so easy for me. I guess that's why I can understand many of the kids who come to fence at the club. Many of them are not team players, but fencing does give them a sense of belonging. Fencing is perfect for people like me. I was lucky to have found it at such an early age."

He suddenly raised his hand and called the waitress.

"Check please," he said when she approached, and took a twenty-dollar bill out of his pocket.

"Anyway, it was really nice seeing you again," he said to me and shook my hand. "Thanks for coming to meet me."

"No problem," I mumbled.

"Keep the change," he said to the waitress as he turned to walk out.

I was left sitting there, thinking: *What the hell was that all about?*

As I made my way home on the subway, my fingers already started to itch. Images were floating in my mind, and I had to stop myself from scribbling on the back of an old leaflet I'd found in my handbag, because I knew I had to get out on the next stop. I could hardly wait to get back home and sit in front of my computer again.

Twelve

The following Sunday the schoolteacher called again. He arrived mid-afternoon, on a gloriously sunny day. Adele and Louis were out in the garden, playing *La Grace*. They took turns throwing the rings which – although not nicely decorated like the ones Adele had seen in the Bertrand shop – did their job just fine. Louis wouldn't normally be caught dead playing *La Grace* with his sister, it was such a girly game. But his best friend Jacques, whom he usually spent Sunday afternoons with, roaming around the village, was helping his father fix a hole in the roof. The two boys studied with the local curé during the week, but Jacques showed far more brilliance than Louis, and therefore was a natural candidate for a place in a school in Lyon, if a place and funding became available. Louis did not excel and was not particularly interested in his studies, and the Padre said to his father he would do well to find him an apprenticeship in Gex, perhaps with one of the local artisans. Jean Durand, who was a potato and maize farmer himself but hoped for a better life for his son, agreed. He had promised Anne, when they married twenty years earlier, that he would make sure their children had a good future. He himself could not understand what was wrong with a life of farming, as his father and father's father had also been farmers and had done just fine – the family never went hungry. But when Anne – the daughter of a well-off leather-worker and bookbinder – agreed to marry him, leave her parents' home near Lyon and move into his humble family home in Chevry, he knew that he would have to make some compromises, and letting his son become an artisan could be seen as one of them.

Jean Durand loved the soil and was a natural early riser – up before the roosters every morning, including Sunday – and there was nothing he enjoyed more than a bowl of stew and a good rest at the end of a hard day of physical labor. His potatoes and maize earned him enough to put food on his family's table, and his physical size and strength became a legend in the village. It was told that he had once lifted a carriage on his own when some poor driver ended up in a ditch and had his legs crushed underneath it. But his son seemed to have inherited the lazy disposition of his wife's family and did not like physical labor.

"Sadly, he does not seem to have the brain or temperament for studying either," commented his own mother. She made it her business to try and motivate her son to get well-paying work. After all, he *was* her only son. She even agreed that they'd send him away to Lyon as an apprentice if he did not show more motivation to work hard, as no local artisan would take on a boy who showed more interest in climbing a tree and daydreaming on the top branch than in learning a *metier*.

But on that specific Sunday the entire family took the day off. Jean Durand's idea of a day off was to go and help his neighbors repair the leak in the roof of their barn, for he could not stand an idle afternoon. The children were allowed to play outside while Anne Durand cut patterns for Adele's party dress, laying them one next to the other, to make sure they were right before she used them as models for cutting the actual fabric.

And so, Louis reluctantly agreed to throw the wooden rings at Adele, and she ran around trying to catch them on the rods she held, one in each hand. Her face was red and sweaty from running around in the sun, and half of her curls had escaped from the hair-tie and bounced on her face every time she jumped to catch a ring.

"Throw it at me, not over my head, Louis!" she yelled at him, frustrated.

"If you don't like the way I play, you can play on your own!" he yelled back.

That was when Jules Badeau showed up, accompanied by Adele's mother, in the back garden.

"We have a visitor, children," she called to them and when Adele saw the tall, slim man standing next to her mother, her knees buckled and her heart skipped a beat.

She dropped the two catching rods to the ground and caught her rebellious curls with both hands, trying to stuff them back into the ribbon that held most of her hair back. Louis looked at her and laughed out loud.

"Shut up," she hissed at him, then smiled sweetly.

"*Bonjour, Monsieur Badeau,*" she called out. "Would you like to play *La Grace* with us?"

He approached them, walking the short distance from the house to the garden with an amused look on his face.

"I will get something for you all to drink," called Anne Durand and disappeared back into the cool house. She didn't like the hot sun, and always said Adele should avoid it too if she didn't want her skin to be as dark as a peasant's.

"*Bonjour, Louis.*" He addressed the boy first, as if used to dealing with boys.

"*Bonjour, monsieur,*" answered Louis and looked down, suddenly embarrassed by the older man's presence.

He then turned his gaze to Adele.

"*Bonjour, Adele.*"

Adele smiled at him, not sure what to say, as she had already greeted him. They all stood in awkward silence for a moment. It was Adele who finally broke it.

"So, would you like to play *La Grace* with us?"

The schoolteacher laughed. "All right, if this makes you happy. It must be at least ten years since I last played this game, with my own sister. I used to be quite good at it, you know."

Adele took this as a challenge. "All right then, you hold this!" She picked up the two rods from the ground and handed them to Monsieur Badeau. She then snatched the other two rods and the throwing rings from Louis' hands.

Jules Badeau took his hat and jacket off, folded the jacket neatly and lay it with his hat on the ground. He then stood in his white shirt a short distance from Adele.

"Ready?" she called, and quickly crossed her own rods, making each ring fly towards the schoolteacher.

Within seconds, the air filled with laughter as he caught ring after ring on his two rods. Louis, encouraged by the presence of an older man who did not mind making a fool of himself by playing a girls' game, joined in and took the two rods from Adele. It was then Monsieur Badeau's turn to throw the rings at Louis, who missed them all, but one.

"Got to practice to be graceful, Louis," joked the schoolteacher. This game was supposed to help teach girls and young women make graceful movements – it was not a boys' game – but it was fun.

Madame Durand called them inside the house for a refreshing drink, and Adele gathered her skirt and led the way into the kitchen, where her mother had prepared a chilled herbal concoction for them to gulp down in big slurps. Adele, of course, was expected to drink it in small ladylike sips, despite her great thirst.

"It is very nice of you to come by, Monsieur Badeau," said Madame Durand. "It is such a beautiful day for a walk."

"Indeed, *madame*," said the schoolteacher. "And such a lovely walk from Gex to Chevry. My dog enjoys it – and so do I."

"Just as well you are here, I meant to send you an invitation to Adele's birthday party next month," said Anne.

Adele felt her cheeks turning red. *Yes, I am happy that my mother is inviting Monsieur Badeau, but shouldn't I be consulted first? She thought.*

"Adele will be turning eighteen and we will be having a small celebration in the village, in Monsieur and Madame Montague's barn, with dancing and all," continued her mother.

"That sounds wonderful," said Monsieur Badeau. "I would love to come, if Adele wants to invite me, that is."

He looked at Adele to see her reaction, but she kept her eyes down on the floor.

"She's just being stroppy because she did not get the dress she wanted," contributed Louis, suddenly taking interest in the conversation. "She should be grateful that she got a new dress at all. Of course, she wanted to have the most expensive fabric in the Bertrand shop."

"Louis!" his mother scolded. "*Occupe toi de tes onions*, mind your own business, will you? Adele will have a beautiful dress, have no doubt. I am making it myself."

She pointed towards the half-finished patterns and the mustardy-yellow fabric, neatly folded on a chair.

"I am certain the dress you are making will look stunning on your daughter, *madame*," said Monsieur Badeau.

"Yes, *Maman*, but you said she wanted the other fabric, the expensive blue-gray one which was beautiful but not practical," continued Louis.

"Enough," said his mother. "Why don't you go back outside? In fact, why don't the three of you go for a walk here in the village, it is such a beautiful day."

"Perhaps another time," said Jules Badeau. "I need to get back now, I do not wish to impose. I just thought I would come by and say hello."

"Very well then," said Madame Durand. "Louis and Adele can accompany you some of the way, it will do them good. Lazing around the house gets them into trouble and causes them to argue with each other. Unless you prefer to peel some potatoes for dinner, Adele, in which case Louis can accompany Monsieur Badeau."

"I am happy to go for a short walk, *Maman*," said Adele in a low voice, almost a whisper. "I will peel the potatoes when I come back."

"Very well, then," said Madame Durand. "Have a good walk back, Monsieur Badeau, and thank you for coming by. I hope to see you again soon."

"Thank you, *madame*," said the schoolteacher, putting his vest back on and his hat on his head. "*Bon Dimanche*, have a good Sunday."

Thirteen

The alarm clock threw me out of my dream, and the details started fading fast. I tried to hold on to them but they were like smoke, twirling around my head and then vanishing. Yet I knew I'd dreamt of Adele again. It was after spending three hours on my computer, writing an entire chapter, as if someone was dictating it to me. I brushed my teeth and collapsed on my bed, exhausted, and I slept through the night – once more.

Then my strange encounter with Noah the previous afternoon floated back into my mind. Why did this person suddenly come into my life? Was the timing coincidental or did it hold some kind of meaning I was supposed to understand?

Am I losing it, I wondered. *This is exactly the kind of thing Lauren would say.*

I decided to schedule another appointment with the hypnotherapist; perhaps I could get some answers to the many questions that I suddenly had. This woman must have done something right, as it was the third night in a row I'd been sleeping for over eight hours, and waking up feeling...feeling energized. Feeling interested in things around me...interested in life. This was refreshing, after the many months of feeling down, perhaps even depressed.

I picked a bright red jacket to wear to the office – and tied a bright yellow scarf around my neck – because life suddenly seemed full of color. I could not explain why, or how, the monochrome of my daily shuffling about, from home to office and back with my paper-filled leather briefcase, had suddenly turned into walking with a bounce in my step. I didn't know the why and the how, but all that mattered was that it had and I was glad. And if it meant more hypnotherapy sessions to try to gain deeper understanding about how my mind – and my life – worked, then so be it.

I called Tatiana as soon as I got into the office, and left a message. Then I started looking through the books that had arrived that week, trying to pick something that looked interesting enough to examine before I decided which foreign publishers to contact. I also had a pile of manuscripts that somehow had ended up on my desk – we called it the slush pile. Going through it was like mining for a diamond in a pool of black water – it was possible that the next bestselling novel would be coming from a manuscript hiding in this pile – but it was highly unlikely.

I did feel obliged to pull out a manuscript once in a while, and to start reading. If the first paragraph was full of typos, it went straight into the recycling bin. But if I could get through the first page and it held my attention, I then wrote a brief email to the author thanking him for sending it in, and wishing him luck elsewhere. Three times in the last fifteen years I actually read an entire manuscript from the slush pile, and we did end up publishing one – but that was seven years ago, when publishing was in a slightly better state. Now I pulled out one that didn't look too bad, but then the phone rang – and it was Tatiana, the hypnotherapist.

She had a cancellation for that afternoon, she said. Would I like to come in?

"Of course I would," I said. "I need to know what happens next."

It was all for the sake of research for my novel, of course.

As I made my way to her practice I tried to prepare myself mentally. I was hoping for some answers, for clarification of some kind. Why were Adele and her life story haunting me?

As I raised my hand to knock on the door, I stopped and examined the dragonfly sticker again. It was an artistic representation of a dragonfly, with a black contour and colorful wings that were blue at the tips, turning yellow towards the center. I was startled when the door opened and the Tatiana stood behind it, a smile on her face.

"Please come in," she said. I did.

"Are you reconsidering?" she asked gently. "Because if you are, you're not the first one. But there's nothing to be afraid of."

"I've had a really strange few days, following our last session," I said as I sat in the leather armchair. "I've had...I am not sure what to call them. Dreams? Visions?"

She looked at me with a kind, but amused expression. "So what would you like to do today?" she asked. "Intent is most important in hypnotherapy. Especially in past-life regressions, if that is what you are aiming for. If you don't know where you want to go, it would be like taking a journey without a clear destination. You'll be getting somewhere, but not necessarily where you wanted to be."

"Interesting," I said. "Is this what you think it was, a past life? And if we do a past-life regression...can't I get stuck in it? Are there any risks?"

"Our intent last time was to help you with your insomnia and anxieties," she said, looking at her file. "Did it help in any way?"

"I've been sleeping for eight to ten hours the last few nights," I said. "I am truly amazed."

"I am so glad it worked, then," she said. "So now you are considering a past-life regression and are worried about the risks, if I understand correctly?"

I nodded. I felt as if I'd opened my heart to this woman, and whatever she would say next might influence not only what would happen in the next hour or two, but possibly the rest of my life.

Tatiana put her pen down.

"A past-life regression is just a journey to some different parts of your subconscious," she said. "You are in full control, you cannot get stuck. You will be aware of what is going on in the room around you, and you can come out of it at any time. You might experience, feel, hear or see things in your mind's eye, if you allow yourself. It is not very different from the state of consciousness you are in just before you fall asleep, or just after you've woken in the morning but are not fully awake yet. Does this make sense?"

I nodded again.

"So, shall we set the intent as the past-life regression experience that is most helpful and relevant to your life at the moment?" she suggested.

"Yes," I said. "That would be great."

"Ok then," she said. "Please lie down and take a few deep breaths. I'll be right with you."

As I lay on her therapist's bed, I closed my eyes and prepared myself for seeing Adele and her life again. Maybe this would help me understand more about her connection to me, if there was one. Or at least would give me ideas for the next chapter in my novel.

I felt Tatiana covering me with a warm blanket.

"I will count down from ten to one..." she started in a quiet voice – and then I was gone.

Fourteen

He lived on the outskirts. He did not like to go into the village but could see it from his hut; it often looked to him like some sort of an illusion – partly real, partly imaginary. The people walking about, tending to their daily chores, were like little floating dots, hovering randomly, unaware of the bigger picture. They only came to him when they needed something: a cure or a blessing. On rare and special occasions, someone asked for a curse.

He did not like to perform the latter. Delivering a curse felt like it went against the very grain of his being, against his natural ways. Yet, he did it every now and then, when he believed it might be justified.

His only company when clients did not come to see him was his ancestors. Their presence was always comforting and pleasant to him – they were not frightening, or stubborn, or ridiculous like some humans were. They were never mean or short-tempered. He felt more comfortable in their presence than in that of the village people, or of those who walked for entire days, or rowed for hours down the river, just to come and see him. He was a well-known healer and sorcerer in this area – admired and feared by many.

There was one thing he never felt and was not sure he would in his lifetime, and that was absolutely fine with him. He never felt loved.

Now there is a woman approaching, a baby tied to her back. She emerges in front of his eyes as if coming out from a cloud of mist. Is she real? Is she not? He decides she is real the moment he notices that in her hands she carries something wrapped in cloth, maybe an offering to him. As she gets nearer he can see the details – her ashen face and sunken eyes.

"My child," he says. She is a child indeed, her skin fresh despite the sadness in her eyes and the smell she brings is that of cooking-fire and fragrant herbs. "What can I help you with?"

She utters a guttural sound, like a wounded animal, as her fingers start undoing the knot on the fabric tied beneath her bosom. She lets the two parts of the fabric slip and he catches the small child behind her back, holding onto its scrawny bottom.

He takes the infant in his arms and sits cross-legged. He then closes his eyes and starts humming. The sound comes from the pit of his stomach and his body rocks backward and forward to a melody that he can hear in his mind. A stream of words that has no meaning to the young mother standing in front of him slips through his lips, giving his face a grim appearance as he starts talking in tongues. The sounds coming out of his mouth make no sense to him, or to the mother, but they do seem to make sense to some small creatures gathering around him and watching with curiosity. A lizard, a few birds, a small monkey with beady black eyes peeking out of the branches where it feels safe enough to hide and try to aim a nut or two at the young woman sitting underneath.

This goes on for some time, and the mother watches him while he rocks her infant son in his arms. At first, she breathes heavily, her mind filled with worry. But then, as the chanting goes on she appears to be giving in to a sensation that envelops her like a cool breeze; to a knowing that descends on her when she looks at the healer's calm face.

"Here you go," he says after what seems like forever, but in reality is no more than a small fraction of time passing. He hands her the child, whose small chest now visibly rises with every breath.

The healer gets up and goes into his hut, emerging a few

moments later with two animal-skin bags. He dips his middle finger into the smaller sachet and when he takes it out, it is covered in thin, white powder. He marks three horizontal lines on the child's forehead.

"For protection," he tells the young mother. She nods.

He then puts his hand into the larger bag and takes out a fist full of herbs. He rolls the herbs in a small cloth and gives the young woman exact instructions as to how to prepare them for the boy. She nods silently.

"Come back to me after three moons," he says.

She nods again, silently putting a small offering at his feet. She then swings the child onto her back and fastens the long piece of fabric under her bosom again. She takes a few steps backwards, as if not wanting to turn her back to the healer. He can feel her apprehension, mixed with gratitude. He is used to this; he has become familiar with the vibrations he senses – whenever he does an act of healing for someone, how they are grateful, but fearful. Fearful of him and of his powers. Yet he knows these powers are not his own; they are only borrowed powers. These are merely powers that he has access to but that are also harmful if not used correctly. Every time he calls on his forefathers and on his spirit guides for help, he imagines himself as a hollow branch, a tube through which these powers flow – through him and onto the person who needs healing. And when he calls they always come, his forefathers and his spirit guides, offering advice and healing.

He is deep in his thoughts when he notices that the woman is still there, looking at him from a short distance away.

He stares at her when he suddenly feels something he can only think of as tenderness flow from her to him. This is something he is not used to. Respect? Yes. Fear? Of course. But tenderness is a feeling he had not experienced very often. It makes him uncomfortable. And there is something else, not tangible, nothing he can put his fingers on, but he just knows that this feeling of *déjà vu* is because this has already happened before.

Maybe in one of my dreams, he thinks. Having premonitions and feelings of *déjà vu* are not a rare occurrence for him, that much he knows. In fact, they feel like second nature, but at the same time are still a bit eerie every time they happen.

The woman keeps looking at him, seeming reluctant to leave. Maybe she doesn't understand him?

He raises three fingers at her.

"In three moons," he repeats. "Now you must go."

And she does; she turns around and walks away carrying the sleeping infant on her back as if it was a rag-doll.

Three moons later she returns. He can hear her before he sees her, the child on her back squealing in delight. It is late afternoon and the sun is beginning its descent behind the trees. The leaves rustle as small animals and large birds make their presence known to him in a cacophony of screeches and songs. He is never a threat to them. His sustenance always comes from gifts people bring. He has no need to hunt. On his daily expeditions to the nearby forest, he gathers medicinal plants and roots – some of the roots he boils and eats. He knows them well by now, can tell the ones that give him strange dreams from the ones that fill his stomach and sometimes make him feel bloated. Every once in a while he gets an offering of meat – usually antelope or gnu meat. Someone once brought meat from a monkey, which he did not eat. However, he did use it for one of his rituals.

As the woman draws closer, he can see the child sitting upright on her back, holding onto his mother's shoulders, his little feet kicking the air.

He greets them with a nod and sees the woman smiling at him. Her smile conveys joy, and something else – something he cannot quite understand. He is much better at interpreting energies than sensing real human emotions. There is nothing more to be said, as the child is obviously well. But it is she who has something for him. It is some kind of fragrant stew, made in gratitude for healing her son.

She sets it in front of him and says something. Or at least he thinks she does, as her lips move, but only an animal-like sound comes out. And then he realizes what is strange about her. She is deaf-mute.

He looks at her and then down at the small wooden bowl in front of him. Saliva fills his mouth and he realizes he has not eaten something that smelled so good in a long time. As if reading his mind, the woman nods and takes a few steps back. She motions with her hand to her mouth, telling him to eat.

She then leaves him to eat his meal, and as she walks away he can make out among the squeals of the monkeys and the singing of the birds, the babbling of the young child.

The child can't be deaf, or he would not be making these sounds, he thinks. *But the mother cannot hear her own child's voice.*

He eats a mouthful of deliciously cooked roots and herbs and an unfamiliar joy fills him like water filling the nearby river after the rainy season – it feels plentiful and clear and powerful.

Fifteen

I opened my eyes and looked at Tatiana – then at the room around me. I remembered where I was, of course – but it felt as if I'd just returned from a long journey. Saliva filled my mouth when I recalled the wonderful smell of the stew, the stew that was offered to the medicine man in gratitude for healing the child.

What was that all about? Who was this medicine man? And then I wondered – where was Adele? I came here to try and reconnect with her, not to have another imaginary experience I couldn't understand.

"How are you feeling?" asked Tatiana, and I didn't know what to say.

"I am fine, just very surprised at what I experienced…what happened to Adele? I expected to see her again."

"Remember, we'd set the intention to have an experience that would be most helpful in your life at the moment," she said. "This might be it."

"But…" I started saying. But what? But I wanted to pursue a fantasy, a dream, a figment of my imagination? Since when did I believe in this kind of thing, anyway? Past lives. Ha.

"I can see you are a little unsettled," said Tatiana. "I am sorry you didn't get what you expected, but many times this is actually for the best. Perhaps what you've experienced will bring some deeper meaning into your life right now."

"I just don't get this," I said. "What can be the relevance of an African medicine man to my life at the moment? It just feels like I'm making these things up. Maybe I've watched a movie that came up from my subconscious…who knows."

Tatiana smiled.

"Who knows," she repeated my words. "Here is your

recording – but again, it's best to wait a week or two before you listen to it."

As I walked out into the early-evening air, I had this same sense of exhilaration I'd experienced the previous time I left Tatiana's practice. I had no explanation as to what or why it happened, but it was as if I had just walked out of a shower – an energetic kind of cleansing, that allowed me to see things around me in a different light. As I prepared to cross the road, I instinctively looked to my left, almost expecting a little green car to turn the corner and rush towards me, but the small street was quiet apart from a few pedestrians, making their way home from work. It was early June and the air smelled sweet, a kind of renewal of life and flowers and even birds that could be heard above the noise of the city. I took my cellphone out of my bag and turned it on – for it had been off for the duration of my session with Tatiana. There were three messages – and I listened to them as I walked. Two were from the office – these could wait until tomorrow. But the third was from Jen. She wanted to know whether she could spend the night at Tammy's again, and something about the message bothered me. Jen was only thirteen, so it was perhaps too soon to worry about her getting involved with boys, or more specifically, the wrong sort of boys. But she had had her first period the year before and started wearing lip-gloss shortly after. This was followed by a little mascara every now and then, when she thought I wouldn't notice, and her skirts were getting shorter and shorter. So yes, perhaps there was something to worry about after all and this message just did not feel right, but I wasn't sure whether forbidding her to have a sleepover was the right way to win her confidence.

"Hi, sweetie," I said as she answered her cellphone. "Got your message, I'm on my way home."

"Hi, Mom," she said. "So is it ok if I go to sleep at Tammy's? We have some homework to do for tomorrow."

"Oh," I said. I intended to use the fact that the next day was a school day as an excuse to say 'no' to the sleepover. Now what?

"Sweetie, I'd much rather you worked at our house – could Tammy come to you maybe?"

There was silence on the other end of the line. I could hear her thinking.

"Besides," I added, "I just came back from the hypnotherapist, I had another session. I'd love to tell you about it."

Emotional blackmail – that should work. I knew she was worried about me and wanted to make sure I was feeling ok, and I was. In fact, I was now feeling more than just ok, but I wanted to talk to Jen, to see what was going on in her life. I had the strong feeling that something was indeed going on, and she was not telling.

"Oh, ok then," she said. I could hear the disappointment in her voice. But her concern for me triumphed over whatever else she had in mind – whether it was really just a studying sleepover at Tammy's or something else – at least for now. I breathed deeply.

"Wonderful," I said. "I'll pick up some Chinese takeout on the way home."

"Ok, Mom," she said just before she hung up. "See you soon."

When I got home Jen was in her room, with the door closed. I could hear she was talking on the phone, so I waited. But after ten minutes or so, I knocked on her door. Realizing she was a teenager now, I was careful about respecting her privacy these days.

"I have to go," I heard her say. "My mom's here."

"Hi, Mom," she said as she opened her door.

"Hi, sweetie, let's eat, the food is getting cold. And I'll tell you all about my hypnotherapy session. Where's Tom?"

"Out, of course," she said. "Why is he always allowed to go places?"

I now remembered he'd mentioned the previous day that he'd be going to a friend's house straight from school, and would come home after dinner. I didn't even bother to ask which friend. But then again, I did know Tom could take care of himself.

"He's fifteen," I said. "Almost sixteen."

"And he's a boy, right?" said Jen. I was surprised by the bitterness in her voice.

"Hmmm...," I said. "Come on, let's eat. Is Tammy coming over later?"

"No," said Jen. "She can't."

I wanted to ask how come she couldn't if she, Jen, was supposed to go and study at Tammy's house, but I didn't want to stir things up even more. I told Jen about my session, about the strange medicine man and the deaf-mute woman, about how he saved her baby's life. As we ate our dinner, I could still recall the smell of the fragrant dish the woman brought him, and taste the flavorsome vegetables and roots in it, feel their creamy texture on my tongue. Telling Jen about it was almost like reliving the experience, recalling details that came to my mind as I described what I saw in my mind's eye.

Jen listened to me, but seemed distracted, and after helping me clean up and throwing the takeaway boxes in the recycling bin, she went back to her room.

"Sorry, Mom, I need to study," she said before she closed the door behind her.

"No problem, sweetie," I said to the closed door. "I need to get on with my novel."

And I sat by my computer again, giving my fingers freedom to explore the keys, to lead me back to Adele's life – I still felt somewhat disappointed that she had not shown up in my earlier session. Who was this strange medicine man, with the deaf-mute woman? How were they relevant to my life?

But I pushed them and these questions out of my mind, so I could focus on Adele again.

Sixteen

A week before her eighteenth birthday a package had arrived, neatly wrapped. She found it on the doorstep on a warm Monday morning. Her father must have walked right past it when he left the house earlier. It did not look as if he had stepped right on it, as the paper was straight and nicely fluffed, even if it was slightly damp from the humidity in the morning air.

There was no name on the package, so she did not know who it was for, but as her eighteenth birthday was just a few days away, she hoped with all her heart it might have something to do with her.

"*Maman*, there's a parcel on the doorstep," she called.

"Well, bring it here," her mother called back from the kitchen, and Adele carried it carefully. It felt soft, yet heavy. What could it be?

She laid it down on the wooden counter and ran her finger across the shiny, white ribbon, a ribbon like the one she had from Monsieur Bertrand's shop. It was like the ribbon that he'd tied on the package with her yellow fabric for the dress, the dress that was now nearly ready, hanging in her mother's bedroom as there were still some finishing touches to be made.

"Do you want to open it, or shall I?" asked her mother, and Adele hesitated.

"Is it for me?"

"Your guess is as good as mine, Adele. Strange that there is no name on it. Open it then, let's see what it is."

Adele carefully untied the white ribbon and savored the rustling of the paper; it was like music to her ears. A surprise. She loved surprises!

She unfolded it carefully, and a flash of gray-blue confirmed what she had not even dared hope.

"Oh, *Maman*, look...it's...what...? How come?"

A large piece of her coveted blue-gray fabric, enough fabric to make a whole new dress, was folded into a neat square. It was smoother than she had remembered and more beautiful in the sunlight streaming through the small kitchen window.

Her mother smiled.

"Well, well, well," was all she said, as her smile grew larger.

"What, *Maman*, did you buy this for me? Oh, I don't know what to say..."

"Of course I didn't buy this, Adele. You know very well we cannot afford this fabric. And we certainly cannot afford two dresses."

"But...who...? Was it Pierre... Monsieur Bertrand? Is it, *Maman*?"

"Looks like he has serious intentions after all, Adele. This is expensive fabric. Even if you take away the profit the Bertrands would make on it, it would still be worth at least three livres... Yes, Adele, he would not send this to you if he were not serious."

Adele was not sure what to say.

"What do you mean, *Maman*?" she finally asked.

"I mean, my dear daughter, that you have an admirer with serious intentions and a good situation in life. That is not something to turn your nose up at. Besides, he is handsome, don't you think?"

"Yes, *Maman*, I think Pierre Bertrand is very handsome, but..." She stopped there as she was not sure how to continue. In fact, she was not sure what she really wanted to say. If her mother thought that Pierre Bertrand was really interested in her, in perhaps marrying her, then that would be something quite...quite adventurous, wouldn't it? Being the wife of a well-off merchant, eating on good linen every single day, living an exciting life of travel...going to Paris, maybe even to London... He said he'd take her to Paris, didn't he?

"But what, Adele?"

"But I am not sure if I love him, *Maman*. Yes, he is handsome, but he is not exciting and smart and funny like…"

Her mother waited for her to finish the sentence, but she never did.

"I suppose he is well-off, *Maman*, isn't he? You think it would be a good thing to marry him, don't you?"

Her mother waited a moment before she replied, as if she sensed the weight the words she was about to utter would carry. "Adele, I will tell you something I've never told you before, but you'll be eighteen soon, you should know."

Adele waited silently.

"When I married your father, Adele, I was your age. He was handsome and strong and when I saw him for the first time my heart skipped a beat. He wasn't the smartest of the young men who courted me, and by far not the richest, but I was attracted to his physique, to his strength. And I didn't think that being the wife of a farmer would be any different from being the wife of a bookbinder, like my mother was. But you know what, Adele? I was wrong."

Adele wanted to say something but could not find the words. Was her mother saying she'd made a mistake marrying her father? Oh, if that was the case, that was so romantic, and so…so tragic.

"Don't get me wrong, Adele, I do love your father," her mother started again. "He is a good man, and a good provider. He is a hardworking man. But you know what? I sometimes wonder what life would have been like to have Marie working here all the time, and not just when we have guests. What it would have been like not to constantly have to clean and wash and cook and look after you and your brother. To have a maid, like my mother did. To live in the city. I know I don't often show it, but I miss this life. And this is the life I want for you. Love is wonderful, but it changes with the years. And then you wonder if you made the right choice."

Adele remained quiet, but her thoughts were racing.

"And you think I will have a good life with Pierre Bertrand, *Maman*?" she finally asked.

Her mother was silent again, looking for the right words.

"Do you love the schoolteacher, Adele?"

"I don't know, *Maman*. I think I do. I never felt like that before. He is so serious, and smart, he makes me feel like he understands life, he knows what it is all about. And he is so funny. He makes me laugh. And he is kind. But I don't know much about him, do I? I don't even know if he really likes me. I only have the feeling my heart gives me. But Pierre Bertrand...he is also nice. He is much more handsome. And all the nice things there are in that shop...and he might take me to Paris one day... I so want to go to Paris."

The two women stood in the kitchen, the parcel sitting between them like an unspoken secret.

Anne Durand ran her fingers over the soft fabric, letting them linger for a few seconds. Then she turned her hands and looked at her palms, rough from washing and cleaning and the occasional work in the fields, helping her husband.

"I will not tell you what to do, you are my only daughter and I want you to be happy. But I also want you to have a good life. Maybe be able to look after your parents in their old age," she finally said. "Your schoolteacher does like you, he has come by recently several times, hasn't he? No man does that if he has no interest. And your father is very fond of him. But he is timid and he does not speak his mind. I am not sure if this is a positive quality in a man, for he will lose many good things in life because of this character trait. Men who achieve things have to reach out and take them, have to be able to fight for them."

The tone of her voice was low and bitter, as if she was already resenting this candidate for son-in-law, for all the good things he would not achieve in life for himself, and for her daughter.

"You look sad, *Maman*," said Adele. "There is no reason to be sad – look at this wonderful fabric. Perhaps we should use it to make a dress for you? You have not had a new dress in such a long time."

Seventeen

The next day Jen didn't make it back home until seven, and didn't call to say she'd be late. I got in around six, as usual, and found Tom in his room, in front of his laptop.

"Hi, Mom," he said without raising his eyes to look at me.

"Hi. Where's Jen?" I asked.

"Dunno," said Tom.

"Didn't she call you? Or say anything?"

I checked my own mobile phone – no messages. I then tried dialing Jen's number, but it went straight into her answering system.

I should have spoken to her yesterday evening, when I felt something was not right, I thought to myself. *What now? Where can she be?*

I started making dinner, thinking that if she didn't come back before seven I'd start calling her friends and looking for her, even if this would embarrass her. It was not like her to be so late without letting me know where she was. But then again, she was growing up, and changing from a sweet little girl to a sometimes-grumpy young woman. At thirteen, nearly fourteen now, she thought she could look after herself, but I wasn't so sure. I read enough newspapers and magazines to know that horrible things could happen to young girls left to their own devices. On the other hand, I couldn't treat her like a kid anymore. I didn't want to alienate her. She had had a hard enough time with her father and I splitting up. Don. I resisted the urge to dial his number, to share my concern with him. Of course, I should talk to him about Jen's behavior, about my worries. After all, he was still her father. But I didn't really want to talk to him, to listen to his smug voice letting me know how well he was doing without me.

So I chopped tomatoes and cucumbers for a salad and I fried up some onions, red peppers and chicken for a stir-fry, and all that time I had my mobile next to me, checking every minute or two that there was no missed call or missed message.

At five to seven I decided to start making phone calls, but as I looked up Tammy's number on my mobile phone – I was sure I had it – I heard a key turn in the lock.

Jen walked in, her schoolbag in one hand, her cellphone in the other.

"Hi, Mom," she said as she closed the door behind her.

"Don't 'Hi, Mom' me," I said. I felt the anger climb up my chest and install itself in my throat. I knew I shouldn't let it explode, not when Jen was standing in front of me, with a challenging smile on her face. It was almost as if she was challenging me despite herself, something compelling her to let the raging teenage hormones or some kind of predisposition take over her usually-kind personality.

She didn't answer, and just stood there, looking at me with those lovely green eyes, her father's eyes.

"Please set the table," I then said, making a conscious decision to postpone our conflict until after dinner.

She obediently washed her hands and set the table, while I put the salad and stir-fry into serving bowls.

"Please call Tom," I said quietly. "Tell him we are having dinner together tonight. He can finish his work later, if that's what he's doing."

Tom came out of his room without an argument, to my great surprise. It was as if he felt my bubbling anger and preferred to let his sister take the heat.

We ate silently, and it was only when we were clearing the plates and Jen was loading them into the dishwasher that I brought up the question.

"So, where were you?"

She didn't answer at first, perhaps pretending not to hear my question, but the silence between us was as tangible as her turned back.

"I was at a friend's house," she said in a voice that carried a warning: *Do not ask me who the friend is.* And I didn't. But I resolved to call Don later and tell him that there was something going on with our daughter. I'd call him even if talking to him would make me feel emotional, anxious, and envious of the quick fix he'd found in his life. Even if it would make me feel betrayed and confused by my feelings towards him – how his cynicism annoyed me for years, how I couldn't stand his macho jokes anymore and how relieved I had first felt when we decided to separate. We said we'd remain friends, for the kids' sakes. We said we'd see how it would go if we just parted amicably for a while, and then take it from there.

Within a month, he'd already moved in with Claudette.

"I need to finish some homework," said Jen, shaking me from my thoughts. "Can we talk about this tomorrow, Mom?"

Suddenly the rebellious teenager was out and my sweet little girl was back in.

"Sure," I said.

She hugged me and picked up her backpack that was still on the kitchen floor, and carried it upstairs to her room.

I decided to postpone the phone-call to Don. I could always speak to him the next day. No point in calling now, he would be busy having dinner out or doing something fun that couples do together. I might even be disturbing him in the middle of...I pushed the thought out of my mind.

I sat by my computer instead, begging Adele to come to my rescue, to carry me away from my life, into hers. And the words came, as if dictated by a mysterious voice inside my head.

Eighteen

It was the morning of her eighteenth birthday, and Adele could hardly contain her excitement. The previous night had been similar – thoughts had rattled in her head like a bag of stones. Who would come? Would Pierre Bertrand be there? Would Monsieur Badeau come? She had not seen him over the past couple of weeks, despite seeing him every single weekend since he'd found her up in the mountains and accompanied her back home. And then, two weeks ago, he stopped coming. She was so keen to see his kind face again, that she actually felt a pain in her stomach, a sensation of longing and sorrow, when she thought he might not show up tonight. She liked to spend time with him, she enjoyed the short exchanges they had – he always impressed her with his quick wit and interesting stories. But there was also something unreachable about him – as if he always kept a safe distance from her. And so, she also hoped Pierre Bertrand would come.

She wanted to see him outside the familiar surroundings of his shop, see if he could dance, if he could make her laugh like Jules Badeau did. She wanted to see what fashionable clothes he'd be wearing.

As for herself, she knew she'd look stunning in her mustardy-yellow dress. Her mother had sewn layers of lace around the collar and the rim of the dress, and this gave it a deliciously festive look, something that was almost too good to be worn at a village fête. The sleeves fit snugly over the arms and then cascaded down to her wrists in a thin but voluminous layer of fabric, and her mother added three flower decorations on the lower back – a small but delicate detail which made Adele feel wonderful when she slipped her new dress on. Her mother was also right about the color – it made Adele look radiant. She had tried her dress on the previous night. Her mother also gave her a box of rouge for her birthday and Adele practiced applying the rouge on her cheeks with a wet bit of wool, in front of the mirror in her room. The young woman looking back at her looked so grown up, so – what was the word Pierre Bertrand had used to describe the blue-gray fabric? Sophisticated.

That lovely, soft blue-gray fabric. Her mother refused to use it for herself, and instead folded it neatly and stored it at the top of Adele's cupboard.

"You will use it one day," she said to her. "There's no rush of making it into a dress now, you just got a new dress. But you should send him a thank-you note."

"I will, *Maman*," said Adele, but in all the excitement of the preparations for her party she forgot to do it. In fact, she didn't really forget, she postponed the act of writing the note time and time again, because she was somewhat embarrassed by her own handwriting. It was clear enough but not as pretty as she wished it would be. She spent hours by lamplight practicing the different letters, tracing them again and again, but they always looked a bit crushed, especially the round letters, the a's and the o's and the d's. They were not as pretty as the letters her fourteen-year-old brother scribbled in his notebook.

Despite the fact he was not as clever as Adele (even her mother admitted to this), he was much better than her at reading and writing. Obviously, thought Adele. He had more practice. She would have loved to spend the entire day reading, or writing in her journal, but never got the chance except for the two or three times in her life when she was sick and stayed in bed.

Never mind, she thought as she got out of bed that morning. *At least I'll get to have a great time tonight. It will not be a Parisian ball, but it will certainly be...exciting.*

Madame Montague's barn looked festive with the colored paper chains hanging from its wooden beams. Other neighbors from the village, happy for the opportunity to party, had brought in a few long wooden tables. On some of the tables stood little flowerpots, delicately decorated by hand.

"These look like they came from the *provence*," commented Adele as she touched one.

Mme. Montague smiled at her.

"I am sure they did," she said, her voice down to a whisper. "But they also come from your admirer."

"*Ah, oui?*" said Adele, one arched eyebrow rising in surprise.

"*Oui, ma belle.* They arrived this morning by carriage from Gex, with a note from Monsieur Bertrand. He thanked me for hosting the party for you and wrote that he is looking forward to seeing us all tonight. He wrote that he will also be bringing some fresh flowers to put in the vases. What a charming young man."

"Oh, so he will be coming tonight!" exclaimed Adele.

Madame Montague smiled at her again.

"I am sure he would not miss your party, Adele. You are a very lucky girl, I hope you know that."

Adele nodded, the yellow ribbon her mother just tied in her hair bobbing up and down.

"Yes, I suppose I am," she said.

The guests started arriving and the warm evening breeze, mixed with the local red wine, put everyone in a relaxed mood. Eugénie and Françoise, Adele's girlfriends, stood at her side while she admired the fresh flowers that Pierre Bertrand brought. There were not any old fresh flowers, but wonderful yellow roses. Adele smiled to herself as she wondered if he intentionally chose the color yellow to go with her dress. After all, he had witnessed the argument with her mother over the fabric in his shop and perhaps thought that yellow flowers would complement the dress she'd be wearing.

"I don't know how he got these roses, but they must have cost a fortune," whispered Françoise. "You are so lucky, Adele."

The three girls looked at Pierre Bertrand, who stood with the other men, drinking wine and laughing. They could not hear what the joke was, but it seemed as if it was at his expense. One of the older men tapped him on the shoulder and Adele noticed his handsome dark-beige jacket.

This is not a man who would be happy doing manual work, she thought. Despite the obvious difference in status, Pierre Bertrand seemed at ease with the village people, some of them rough farmers who still had dirt on their hands from a week of labor in their fields. While the women huddled in the corner, cutting quiches and fussing over cakes, the men engaged in political debate which, fueled by alcohol, became louder and louder by the minute.

"Here's to the king and his *petite poissonade*, his little fish-stew!" called Monsieur Montague, and the others lifted their glasses.

"*Santé!*" they called out, and emptied their glasses again and again.

"What are they talking about?" whispered Eugénie.

"I don't know," Adele whispered back.

That was when she saw him, and jumped back in surprise.

"*Oh, bonsoir, Monsieur Badeau!*" she said when she saw him smiling at her. As always, he looked slightly amused.

"*Bonsoir, Adele*," he answered, and Françoise and Eugénie giggled next to her.

"Please meet my friends, Monsieur Badeau. This is Eugénie, and this is Françoise."

"Enchanté," said Monsieur Badeau and the two girls giggled again.

"I didn't see you," said Adele. "When did you arrive?"

"Just now. I came this way," he said, pointing to the path leading from Gex through the fields. "It is such a nice evening for a walk. And for a party, of course. I see the other gentlemen started drinking a while back," he added, pointing his chin towards some of the merry men who continued talking loudly.

"What is the king's *poissonade*, Monsieur Badeau?" asked Adele and shoved her elbow in Eugénie's ribs, to stop her silly giggling. She really wanted to know, and suspected the school-teacher would be able to enlighten her.

Jules Badeau laughed, and she noticed a sparkle in his dark eyes.

"Where did you hear this, Adele?"

Adele pointed at the group of loud men.

"We heard them drinking to the king and his *poissonade*. Does the king like fish-stew, Monsieur Badeau?"

"They refer to the king's..." he hesitated for a moment. "They refer to the king's lover, Adele, his *amoureuse*. Her name is Jeanne-Antoinette Poisson. They are making fun of this relationship."

"Oh," said Adele, blushing. "I see."

"In fact, sounds like she is quite a remarkable woman," said the schoolteacher. "Yes, she is a commoner, but she is well educated and apparently quite clever, too. She is also said to be very good-looking," he added. Now it was his turn to blush a little.

"And this Mademoiselle Poisson, she is the king's mistress?"

"Yes, Adele, this is what gossip says. In fact, it is quite well known, I suppose. But it is not something a girl your age should be talking about."

Adele stuck her chest out.

"But, Monsieur Badeau, I am eighteen today!"

"Yes, of course. I almost forgot. Happy Birthday," he said and reached into his pocket. He took out a small box and handed it to Adele. She wasn't sure what do to, and his hand was left extended, holding the box, a moment too long.

"You don't want to see what it is?" he asked.

"Oh, yes, Monsieur Badeau, of course. But you shouldn't have..."

"Open it, Adele. It should go well with your new dress."

She took the box and hesitated for a few seconds before opening it. What would she find in it? Maybe an engagement ring? She felt her cheeks flushing at the thought and her heart pounding. She just hoped that Monsieur Badeau, who stood next to her, could not hear it.

She opened the box and saw a small rectangular locket on a thin gold chain. Something was engraved on it – she ran her finger across the engraving and read it out loud.

"July 25, 1751. That is the day I was born. It is so pretty, Monsieur Badeau. *Merci beaucoup.* Thank you."

He smiled at her and tipped his hat at her two girlfriends who stared at him, their mouths open.

"See you later, *mesmoiselles*. I'd better go and greet everyone else."

And with these words he left them and walked towards the group of men.

Nineteen

The images haunted me for the rest of the evening, as I made sure both Tom and Jen did not stay up beyond ten o'clock. It was a school day the next day, and a working day for me, but I could not stop these characters from my novel, Adele and the schoolteacher, Jules Badeau, from constantly whispering in my ear.

Our story waits to be told, they said. *Listen to us. Write it down.*

I got ready for bed and hoped they would show up again, in my dreams. I even had a notebook ready on my bedside table, to write the details down if I could remember them when I woke up in the morning, knowing how fickle images that appear in dreams can be when the first rays of morning sun chase them away.

But as I closed my eyes and waited for them to come and speak to me again that night, they refused my invitation.

Instead, it was *he* who appeared again, filling my mind with images I did not understand.

When the white people arrived, their phantom-like faces filled him with dread. It wasn't fear of the ghostlike, unnatural paleness of their skin, nor of the firearms they carried, which were said to be able to kill an antelope, or a man, from a great distance.

Something from within him, like many times before, gave him the feeling that he knew the outcome of this encounter, and it would not be a positive one.

Someone sent them his way, and when he saw them arriving, a small group of village elders accompanying them, he did not even bother to stand up. He received them sitting under the tree by his hut and looked at them as if they were an ordinary sight.

"Uncle, these people have come a long way," said one of the village elders. "They want to bargain with us."

He knew that the white people's convoy had been spotted the day before making its way downriver, and a small army of youths, armed with their bows and their spears, silently ran alongside their canoes until they moored near the clearing, not far from the village.

The pale faces were frightening for many of the youths, as they looked as if they were painted with white powder; except the powder wouldn't rub off.

The group disembarked and tied their boats to a rock, leaving two African men to guard them. As they made their way towards the village, the young warriors followed them from a safe distance. It was only when they approached the village that a warning arrow was shot, landing with precise accuracy several steps in front of the group of white men.

They stopped in their tracks and looked around them. Two of the men brought their rifles up to their shoulders, but could see no one to shoot at.

"We are here to talk!" called a bearded man. His words fell roughly on the ears of the young warriors. Another arrow landed right by his feet.

They had a translator with them – a tall, slim man from a village two days up the river, and he spoke the white men's language. A strange language it was; it sounded lazy and guttural, as if these people had their tongues tied to the roof of their mouths.

"Stop," he called out. "We come with offerings."

The arrows halted and dark eyes peered at the men between the trees. A slim youth hesitantly emerged from the foliage, his dark eyes blazing in the middle of red, smudged circles of paint on his face. He pointed his bow at the men, his sharp arrow glistening in the sunlight emerging between the leaves. One of the men pointed his rifle at the youth.

The bearded man raised his hand.

"We come in peace!" he said. The translator conveyed the message and the youth lowered his bow. The man, in turn, lowered his gun.

"Ask him to take us to his leader," barked the bearded man at the translator.

The translator did.

Two more youths emerged from the foliage, and led the group towards the village. Six or seven other young men kept at the back, hidden behind the trees, following the group of men like dark shadows. Their bows and spears were at the ready until the very moment the group of men were delivered to the village elders who sat by the stump of the baobab tree, expecting the pale-faced strangers. Then they all ended up by the healer's hut.

"They want to take with them twenty young men," said one of the elders.

The healer said nothing.

"They want to give us many gifts for the help of these men."

The old man remained silent.

A short consultation ensued, and the men tried again.

"They will give you clothes and even some of these things, these weapons," said the translator. "They can help you hunt from a distance."

The healer closed his eyes, then opened them again.

"Tell them to come back in two moons," he said to the translator. "I have to consult the ancestors."

The tall man translated this reply, and the white men exchanged rapid words. One of them barked something back at the translator.

"They say that they cannot return in two moons, that is too long. They will return in one moon to have the answer."

The elders looked at each other with surprise, for they all

knew the ancestors could not be rushed.

Everyone waited for the healer's reply.

"If you so wish," he said. "Come back in one moon. If the ancestors agree, you should have your answer."

The translator conveyed this to the white men, and one of them laughed.

The bearded white man took something shiny out of his bag and handed it to the healer. It was a necklace made of shiny stones, each sparkling like clear water.

The healer took the necklace and examined it carefully. He said a few words to the translator, who seemed reluctant to translate.

"What did he say?" asked the bearded man.

"He says this necklace is pretty and that the moon will reflect in it," said the translator.

"Tell him that there are many more where this came from," said the white man.

"But he also says the reflection of the moon cannot be trusted," said the translator.

The white men looked at each other again.

"Tell him we'll be back tomorrow," said the bearded man.

The healer said something and nodded.

"What did he say?"

"He said: *Beware of the moon, it can be deceiving, especially when reflecting in the river*," said the translator.

The group of white men turned around without another word and headed back to their boats.

After the white men left, the healer got up on his feet and walked into his hut. The elders waited for him outside.

When he emerged, his face was smeared in white powder; dark circles were painted around his eyes.

"I am going to the forest, to meet the ancestors," he said.

"When will you be back?" they asked.

"I will be back after I have heard the ancestors," he answered.

"And if the white men return before then?"

"Then they will wait until the ancestors have spoken."

With that he left and walked slowly away from his hut, away from the river to which the white men had gone, and deeper under the canopy of trees that was full of life and sound and mystery.

Twenty

The next morning I called Don. I felt unsettled even before I dialed his number, and this feeling grew into an unpleasant pressure in my chest as I counted the rings on the other end. He answered on the fourth.

"Yes, Amelia," he said, and I almost hung up. Of course he recognized my cellphone number, I'd had it for the past ten years, maybe more. But did he have to be so businesslike, so bluntly uninterested in what I had to say to him, before he even knew what it was?

I swallowed the urge to speak back to him with the same tone of voice.

"Hi, Don," I said. "I am calling about Jen."

"What's up?" he said. I could hear voices in the background. Probably in a meeting at the architects' firm he was a partner at.

"Is this a bad time?" I asked, knowing that with Don there would never be a good time.

"Just got out of a meeting," he said. "Tell me."

"Well," I started. "She's been acting strange lately. Very secretive, not herself really. And last night she came home late from school, and wouldn't tell me where she had been."

There was a brief silence on the other end.

"She's becoming a teenager," he said.

"Yes, that's exactly why I'm worried. Not quite sure what to do about it. Will you try to talk to her when you pick her up this weekend? Maybe she'll tell you more. After all, she doesn't see you that often. Maybe she'll answer your questions more easily."

"Yeah..." he said. "I wanted to talk to you about that. Claudette and I...we are invited to a party Upstate this weekend, and I was wondering if we could switch weekends. It's not a big deal, right?"

Why would it be a big deal, Don? I just told you I'm worried about our daughter, who obviously is dealing with some issues she will not share with me. I just asked you to do your fucking parent duty and talk to her. Why would it be a big deal? Of course stupid skinny-shouldered Claudette and your party take priority, I thought.

"Of course not," I said. "But please talk to her next weekend, then."

"Sure thing," he said. "Gotta go now, see you the following weekend then. Oh, and will you tell the kids for me?"

"Sure thing," I said, before I hung up.

The conversation reminded me how much I now disliked this man, who I truly believed I loved when we met, some twenty years back, when I had just arrived in New York City. He was a good-looking, tall and confident young man, with a smile that I fell for straight away, when we met at a friend's party in a loft in Greenwich Village. I was living in a shared apartment with three other girls, so we went back to his. We dated on and off for four years, until he proposed to me, a week after I told him I was pregnant. I was flattered, excited, enamored with the idea of calling this handsome guy 'my husband' and having a baby with him. Was I really in love with him back then? It's easy to say that I was, but the honest answer is that I don't really know. It felt as if I had glided into this marriage, and into motherhood, without much thought. As if led by an invisible hand that made it all easy, comfortable, nice. It was almost as if I had no say in it, as if I was following a pre-destined path.

The day at the office was uneventful, although I did manage to secure French translation rights for a book I'd been very enthusiastic about – a novel about a Mexican immigrant arriving in the United States, written by a first-time novelist who had immigrated from Mexico with her family as a young girl. I wanted to be part of making her American dream come true – and being sort of an immigrant myself, although I did feel

American even though I was born in Paris – made this book deal even more important to me. Every little thing I was doing now was suddenly painted in a different light, making me wonder whether I was really making any difference in this world.

Was it my recently crumbling personal life, the not-so-recent crossing of the forties threshold or some kind of spiritual journey I had embarked on without intending to? I didn't know, but what I did know was that things suddenly felt different.

I called Jen twice, once around twelve-thirty, when I thought she might be on her lunch break, and the second time around three, but I got her voicemail both times. I didn't leave a message, although I knew she'd be able to see my missed calls. She would call me back if she wanted to, I didn't want to turn into this harassing mom who didn't give her daughter enough space to breathe.

On the way home, on the subway, I consciously tried to stop thinking about Don, and about Jen. The hollow feeling these thoughts made me feel in the pit of my stomach went away. That was when I started thinking about Adele again, and how I would go home, make dinner, try to convince my kids to eat around the dinner table instead of eating in their rooms in front of their computer screens, and then sit in front of my own computer screen and continue writing. And if Jen and Tom preferred to eat their dinner in their room, as has been the case so many times over the last few months, well then, I would just let them. And I would eat something quickly and then do what my mind and my heart were really pushing me to engage in this evening, what my fingers itched to do – to type down more of Adele's story on the keyboard, take it out of my mind where it now seemed to flow without interference and onto the computer screen, birth it into the world.

Twenty-One

As the sun had set behind the Jura and the air got cooler and drier, preparations were made for dancing to begin. Someone brought out an accordion and someone else had a flute, and they started playing quick, cheerful tunes while the women cleared away the platters of food. At first everyone tapped their feet to the beat of the music. But very soon Madame Montague grabbed her husband's hand and pulled him to the center of the circle and they both happily – and slightly drunkenly – did a few *promenade* steps, more or less to the rhythm of the accordion. They were immediately joined by a few other couples, the younger girls dancing with each other.

"Shall we?"

Adele was taken by surprise when Pierre Bertrand extended a hand to her. She put her hand in his and he pulled her into the circle. Her two friends giggled and followed them, dancing with each other alongside Adele and Pierre. The accordion wailed and the dancers swirled and Adele could not wipe the smile off her face. Pierre Bertrand's eyes shone with enthusiasm and joy as he danced with her. They moved in coordination a couple of steps from each other, not quite touching, until he took her hand again and walked around her, spinning her slowly. She noticed other dancing couples smiling at them and she smiled back. This felt so good!

For a brief moment a thought about the schoolteacher crossed her mind and she tried to turn her head and catch a glimpse of him, see if he was watching her dance with Pierre Bertrand. She felt a mix of excitement about dancing like this and worry that Jules Badeau might be taking it the wrong way. But then she thought, *Good, perhaps he will even be jealous.* That thought made her stomach swirl with agitation. She did catch a glimpse of the schoolteacher, standing in the semi-darkness on his own, drinking from a cup and looking at her. *Was he drinking wine?* The insignificant thought popped in and out of her head as their eyes met for a brief moment. Then Pierre Bertrand spun her around and they drifted among the other dancers and Adele forgot all about the schoolteacher for a while longer. When the music stopped and the musicians took a break, Pierre Bertrand kissed her hand and thanked her for dancing with him. Adele blushed and joined Françoise and Eugénie, who were both grinning.

"He's a good dancer," said Eugénie. "You're lucky."

"And he's really good-looking, Adele," said Françoise.

Adele smiled.

"He is, isn't he? But I don't know that he would take someone like me seriously, his family is so well off... They probably expect him to marry some other merchant's daughter..."

"I don't know," said Françoise. "He seems to really like you."

"You're lucky," said Eugénie again. "Everyone seems to like you, Adele. That schoolteacher...he likes you, too."

"You think so? He is so..." Adele looked for the right words. "He is a bit strange, don't you think? He can be so distant and distracted. He treats me as if I were a child. I don't know if he is my type."

As she spoke the words, something inside her rebelled, as if she knew she was deceiving her friends, and perhaps even herself. She did like the schoolteacher. She liked him so very much. But she also liked dancing, and flowers, and nice clothes. And he was not one who would care for such things, was he?

"Well, he left when he saw you dancing with Pierre Bertrand," said Françoise, and pointed in the direction of the now-dark footpath to Gex.

Adele looked in that direction, suddenly feeling sad.

"What's up?" asked Françoise.

"Nothing…" said Adele. "I don't know…"

"Oh, Adele, a man not willing to overcome a few obstacles for you, to fight for you, is not worthy of you," said Eugénie. "Besides, you just said he was not your type."

Adele nodded. The accordion started wailing again, as the musicians ended their alcohol-infused break and resumed playing.

"You're probably right," she said. "Let's go and dance some more."

Twenty-Two

Jen was not happy when I told her that her father would not be picking her up on Saturday morning. Tom didn't seem to care as much.

"Whatever," he said.

"I guess he cares more about her than he cares about us," said Jen.

"It's not that, sweetie," I said. "It's just that they have a party Upstate this weekend and it would be difficult to…" I stopped right there. I didn't sound convincing even in my own ears.

I could see the tears welling up in Jen's eyes. Tom just got off the sofa and walked to his room, closing the door behind him.

"Let's do something nice together this weekend," I said. "Something we've never done before. Something that would be fun for you."

Jen shrugged.

"Maybe shopping?" I suggested. "Or we could go to a movie? A restaurant? Just tell me what you'd like and we'll do it. Even if Tom is busy, or doesn't want to come along, we'll do it together. It'll be just you and me. We haven't done something together for a while."

Jen's face suddenly brightened up. "I know," she said.

"What?"

"Well," she started. "There's this guy…"

I waited patiently, hoping with all my heart that this would be the opportunity for her to open up, to trust me and tell me things, tell me what's been on her mind lately. And I needed to make sure I deserved that trust, not say something rushed or stupid or that would make her clam up.

"There's this guy at school," she then said. "I really like him, but he doesn't even notice me. He hangs out with all the sporty kids, and I'm kind of a nerd, right?"

"No you're not," I said. I wasn't sure if I was completely ready to have this woman-to-woman talk with my thirteen-year-old daughter, but I was willing to give it my best shot.

"So you'd like to go and get a haircut maybe? Something that would draw more attention to your gorgeous eyes? Or we could even go and get you some cool clothes for school, something really…"

"Mom," she interrupted me. "I don't think he's into that kind of stuff. You know, he's into sports. He's training like five times a week and never hangs around after school because he's always training."

"Oh," I said. I decided to let her speak and not ruin the moment with my irrelevant suggestions.

"So I thought…" she started again, "Maybe on Saturday I'll go to where he trains, and hang out…maybe I'll see him there…and it could be fun to try a new sport, too. You always say I spend too much time at home in front of my computer, right?"

I nodded.

"Sounds like a good idea," I said. "Trying something new is always good. Especially a new sport. I am happy to hang out with you this weekend, even take you there on Saturday if you want, we can spend the day together. Especially if you're willing to try and play football for this guy, or is it hockey? Or basketball?"

I knew these were the three most popular sports at Jen's school, and thought she was brave to try and integrate into a team with something she'd never tried before, something she didn't even have the vaguest interest in before she fell for this kid at her school.

"No, Mom," she said. "I would never want to play football or hockey, or basketball. Not even for a guy. You know I am not a team player."

"What is it then?" I asked.

"Fencing," she said.

At first I thought I hadn't heard her right, but then I felt dizzy, as if some strange twist of fate was meddling with my life, with my relationship with my daughter.

"Really?" I said, not knowing what else to say.

She nodded, enthusiastically. "Yes, Mom, would you call the Manhattan Fencing Center and see if you can book a lesson for me for this weekend? Just to try it. I know he trains there because I followed him after school two days ago. That's why I got home so late. I really wanted to know where he trains. Does that make me a creep, Mom?"

I hugged her, and was happy that she let me.

"Of course not," I said. "People in love do strange things sometimes."

She smiled at me.

"You're the best mom in the world," she said.

Twenty-Three

As Adele took off her now-wrinkled dress and carefully hung it on her cupboard door, she felt her head spinning. It was not from that one glass of wine that she was allowed to drink – until now she had been allowed only small sips from her mother's glass on special occasions – but from fatigue mixed with exhilaration. It had been such an exciting evening; she was so sorry it was now over.

Her mother entered the bedroom and startled her from her thoughts.

"You are going to sleep, right? The sun will be rising soon."

"Yes, *Maman*, I will try. But I don't know if I can."

"Well, you should at least try. Do you want to talk?"

"No…yes…I don't know."

Anne Durand sat on her daughter's bed, and handed the nightgown to her. "Here, put this on and come lie down here, I will sit next to you."

Adele slipped on her long nightgown and then removed her undergarments. She suddenly felt shy about undressing in front of her mother.

"Adele," said Anne Durand, "we will have to make an important decision soon."

Adele stared at her mother. There was no use pretending; it was as if her mother could read her mind.

"I don't know what to do, *Maman*," she finally said.

"That is why I am here, my daughter. To try to make sure you will have a good life. You are actually very lucky to have a choice, many girls don't."

"I don't know that I have a choice, *Maman*. You mean…whether to marry or not?"

"Don't be silly, Adele, of course you will marry. The only question is which husband you will choose. You need to choose a husband who will be able to give you the things you want in life."

"I just want to see things in this world, *Maman*. I want to go to new places, I want to visit Paris and… I am sad to say this, but I don't want to live here all my life, although of course I will come back one day, like all the travelers who come home after exploring the world."

Her mother smiled. "You have such imagination, my girl. But if this is what you want, then you have your answer. And I think you are right."

"You mean, Monsieur Bertrand? Pierre?"

"Oh, so you call him by his first name now."

Adele smiled shyly.

"He said I could call him that…"

"Of course he did. And the other one?"

"You mean Monsieur Badeau?"

"Don't be coy, girl. Yes, I mean Monsieur Badeau. Did he say anything to you? Anything of importance?"

"He gave me this, *Maman*, such a nice birthday present…"

Adele reached for the small box on her night table and handed it to her mother.

Anne Durand opened it and stared at the gold locket.

"It is very pretty, Adele. But you might have to give it back, if you decide to marry the other one."

"It has my date of birth engraved on it, *Maman*. What good would it do to give it back?"

Her mother looked at the engraving and then at Adele. "Indeed. He is a clever man, your schoolteacher. He did not want to give you the option of giving it back. But still, you should. He can always melt it down and sell the gold."

Adele felt a lump in her throat.

"You know, *Maman*, I really like him. Why did he not stay?

Why did he not dance with me?"

Her mother sighed. "I know men like him, Adele. He is a good, clever man. He has a kind heart. Too kind, I would say. He is not one made for business or for adventure."

"But he didn't even ask me to dance. He didn't even put up a fight for my attention, he just left when I danced with Pierre...with Monsieur Bertrand. Did I offend him? But he didn't ask me to dance with him!"

Adele was surprised to feel tears stinging her eyes. "Why did he just leave, *Maman*? Does he not care about me?"

Anne Durand covered her daughter with a soft blanket. Despite the warm summer air, the thick walls of the house made the room feel chilly.

"I think he does care about you, Adele. But perhaps he is a man who will not fight for love. There are men like that. This does not mean they are lesser men; it just means that they control their emotions. They keep their passion well hidden, too well hidden, and a woman has to work hard to unveil it."

"You know, *Maman*, I think that if he were willing to fight for me, to dance with me, to take a risk for me, I would be happy to be with him. I do like him so very much... He is smart, and funny, and...and he saved my life. I think I do love him. But Pierre Bertrand, he is so easygoing, he is fun and handsome and he dances well...it would be an easier life to be married to someone like him, no?"

"I think you are right, Adele, although I will support your wishes when we talk to *Papa*. You know he likes the schoolteacher; he thinks that he is a decent, hardworking man. Which is very true. But you do need to decide, and we will tell *Papa* that you prefer Monsieur Bertrand if this is your wish. Then we can take care of things for you. Otherwise some other lucky girl will get him, and his family will only rejoice if he chooses to marry some well-off young woman. We have to act fast, while his heart is still longing for you."

"*Maman*! Are you saying he will stop loving me? That his feelings for me are temporary?"

"That is the nature of humans, Adele, and especially the nature of young men. If you decide to marry your schoolteacher, Monsieur Bertrand will get over it, have no doubt. There are many girls who would be more than happy to take your place as his wife."

The two women looked at each other silently, all the words they cared to share spoken. Yet the unspoken ones lay in the air like invisible clouds, pregnant with the rain yet to come.

"Go to sleep, Adele, and we will talk to *Papa* later this evening," said Anne Durand as she stood up. She went to the window and drew the curtains shut as the first rays of sun started sneaking into the room, coloring it pale orange and yellow and shimmering beige.

"Sweet dreams, *Maman,* and thank you for this wonderful party," mumbled Adele, pulling the blanket to her chin.

Her mother smiled and shut the door behind her.

Twenty-Four

I called the Manhattan Fencing Center, and asked about a fencing class for Jen. The young woman on the other end of the line was cheerful and polite, and explained that Jen needed to be scheduled for a private lesson and then, if deciding to go ahead, would be placed in the correct class. Once her level had been established, she could do a combination of lessons, classes, camps and boutings.

"Wow," I said. "She'd just like to try it, once."

"No problem," she said. "I have a class available for her on Saturday at two p.m., with Sergey, if that works?"

"Sure," I said. "Thank you."

"Have a great day," said the young woman on the other end, and something about her enthusiasm made me feel as if she'd actually meant it.

I recalled my visit to the Manhattan Fencing Center just the previous weekend, the palpable strength and self-confidence of the youths I saw walking around there. What was the likelihood of my visiting this place again this coming weekend? If it were one of my writers, writing it in one of their novels, I'd say – nah. But this was real life, and I hesitated about seeing Noah again, if he happened to be there on the Saturday afternoon when we were expected for Jen's first private lesson. His appearance, or reappearance, in my life at this time of difficulty felt almost unnatural, as if he had some role still waiting to be played out.

On Saturday morning Jen was up by nine, which was very unusual for her. She took a long time in the shower, and emerged with eyelashes thickened by mascara and lip-gloss on her lips.

"Jen, is this a good idea? You'll be wearing a mask anyway."

She looked at me as if I had just said she should shave her head, and I bit my lip. She was a young woman in love, for the first time. She was bound to make some stupid mistakes, and I couldn't prevent her from making them – I could just be nearby to try and prevent her from getting hurt more than the absolute necessary. We had a good mother-daughter relationship, and I was grateful for it. I wanted to make sure it stayed that way. That she felt that she could confide in me. Even if this meant letting her wear mascara for her first-ever fencing class, with the inevitable result of it smudging everywhere when she sweated under that mask. Some mistakes must be made for life lessons to be learned, and not putting on mascara before practicing an intense sport is one of them.

By the time we had had an early lunch and taken the subway to 42nd street, Jen's eyes were shining with excitement – I had rarely seen her so enthusiastic. The last time I saw such hope in her eyes was probably when we went to Disney World in Florida some six years back, when Don and I were still functional as a couple. That must have been our last big trip as a family, because shortly after that we started taking separate vacations and decided that it was better to keep away from each other than constantly get on each other's nerves.

"Do you even know if he'll be there?" I asked. "What's his name, anyway?"

"Gabriel," she said as if whispering a sacred word. "And he's always there, he's always training. He wants to make it to the Pan American Championship next year."

"Sounds like a very dedicated guy," I said, and watched Jen's face light up.

"Yes, Mom, he's awesome, he really is."

I was happy to see her so happy, and just hoped that this joy of first love would not come crashing down like a tower of sand, on my daughter's heart.

We entered the building and took the elevator to the second floor. It all looked familiar now, which was a strange sensation, but Jen didn't notice the confidence with which I led us both to the front desk.

I watched her eyes grow wide as she took in the shiny blue and gray floor, the photos of Olympians and World-Medalists hanging on the walls all around us. The young people dressed in white and silver. Something about the atmosphere was captivating, almost magnetic.

"You must be Jennifer Rothman." The enthusiastic young woman welcomed us – I recognized her voice from our phone call.

"Yes," said Jen, looking at me. She suddenly had the appearance of an insecure little girl, not the dreamy, confident teen who had walked into the building with me just moments earlier.

"I'll sort you out with gear," said the young woman, "and you can change in there." She pointed towards the changing-rooms. "Your mother can wait here, if she wants, or she can come and get you in an hour."

She was talking to Jen as if I wasn't standing right there, next to her.

I looked at the waiting area, complete with comfortable chairs and a television set broadcasting some kind of fencing video, and resisted the urge to ask about Noah. I then decided I'd take the opportunity and disappear, maybe go have a coffee somewhere and start reading the book I had been carrying around in my handbag for the past week. This was another book on offer for translation rights and I needed to know at least what it was about before I tried to sell it to my Paris-based contacts.

"I'll come and get you in an hour, Jen," I said to her and she grabbed my elbow and gave it a little squeeze.

"Thanks, Mom," she whispered and I couldn't help but smile. So I had done the right thing today, by bringing her here, despite the strange feeling I got about this whole synchronicity thing with fencing, and with this club.

"No problem, sweetie, see you later," I said.

I walked back out into the cloudy New York day and turned the corner to look for a café. Then I remembered the one where I had sat with Noah Welder the previous weekend – or rather the one where he had walked out on me, leaving me sitting in front of my half-empty coffee cup, feeling like an idiot. I decided to go back to that café – the coffee was good – and I was quite sure I would not bump into him there. I didn't think this was his regular place or something – if anything, he was probably back at the Fencing Center, coaching.

I realized, with a little surprise, that I was disappointed that I hadn't seen Noah this morning. He was a strange man, no doubt, but something about him soothed me. He had an unthreatening presence, one that you could expect from a child or an older person, yet he was in no way childish, or old. There was something about him that felt comforting, and baffling at the same time. The fact that he had made the effort to seek me out after he almost ran me over, call me and arrange a meeting and then walked out on me as if I was insignificant made we wonder whether he didn't like me as a middle-aged woman, or whether he really just had a need to close a circle, as he had said the previous weekend. Perhaps our meeting, after twenty-something years of not seeing each other, did serve to close some business for him in the grander scheme of things.

One way or another, I had no urgent need to find out, and by the time I finished my coffee and read a few chapters in the new book – which weren't too bad – it was time to go and get Jen.

I made my way back to the Fencing Center, and up to the second floor. The same young woman at the reception desk greeted me with a pleasant smile, and this time I followed her suggestion and sat on one of the black sofas, my eyes moving involuntarily towards the television hanging on the wall in front of me.

When they disconnected from the television screen, they landed on my daughter standing right in front of me, grinning as if she just got a marriage proposal from her beloved. I was right about the mascara – it was smudged all over her eyelids, but she didn't notice – and if she did, she didn't seem to care.

Right behind her, dressed all in black again, was Noah Welder.

"She looks just like you," he said, as if continuing a conversation we just stopped five minutes ago.

"Hi, Noah," I said.

"Sergey called in sick this morning, so they asked me to take his classes," he said as if answering a question. "Imagine my surprise when I got assigned this one. She's got a natural talent, by the way."

"Really?" I said, and quickly added, "Of course, Jen has many talents."

"Nice to see you again," he said. "Off to teach a class now."

And with that he turned around and left me sitting there on the sofa, with my sweaty, smiling daughter standing in front of me.

"It was awesome, Mom," she said. "Really awesome. I'd like to sign up."

"Sign up for what?"

"For the club, of course. I can come here after school a few times a week and practice."

I didn't know what to say to that. Not that I had anything against my daughter taking up any new sport, but fencing? And here, at this club? Of course, there was the incentive of seeing her crush Gabriel, which was not silly. She was a smart girl.

"Would you like to have more information about our membership, Mrs. Rothman?" The young woman smiled at us from behind the reception desk. She was obviously listening in to our conversation.

"Ah...sure," I said, and got up to approach her.

Twenty minutes later we walked out of the club. I filled in the forms while Jen showered and changed back into her jeans and long-sleeved t-shirt.

"Did you see Gabriel?" I asked.

She shook her head.

"Disappointed?" I asked.

"No, Mom," she grinned. "I'll come back Monday straight from school, I'm sure I'll see him then."

"Did you really enjoy fencing or is it all for Gabriel's sake?" I just had to ask.

"I loved it, Mom," she said enthusiastically. "I really did."

I sighed. I guessed this was a good thing, but for some reason, it felt strange, almost pre-arranged, as if events were unfolding according to some invisible plan that was beyond my comprehension. But if this made Jen happy, I would support her and not stand in her way, even if this membership and beginner's fencing package just made our bank account several hundreds of dollars slimmer. Hopefully Don would agree to help with some of the costs. After all, it was his weekend in the joint custody agreement, and if he'd come and got the kids as planned instead of going to some fancy party Upstate with his fancy Claudette, events would have probably unfolded otherwise.

Twenty-Five

"So what did he say when you gave him back the necklace, *Maman*?"

Anne Durand looked at her daughter for a moment without saying a word.

"*Maman*, please tell me."

"He said nothing."

"Nothing? Nothing at all?"

"He said nothing, Adele. But what did you expect him to say? It's a done deal. You are now officially engaged. You should not be keeping such a precious gift from another man."

Adele felt tears stinging her eyes.

"But how come he said nothing? He could have said...he could have... I don't know, *Maman*."

"I told you, Adele, men like Monsieur Badeau don't express their feelings to the world. They keep to themselves and sort out their own issues. He is not an outgoing man and you would have had to work hard to get him to show his feelings. He is not like you; you are open and outgoing. So is your future husband, might I add. And you've made your decision. So forget about Jules Badeau now, and get on with your life – your new life, might I add."

Adele could not explain her sadness, not to her mother and not even to herself. She felt as if a part of her had gone forever, as if someone had cut out a slice of her heart and now there was an empty pit where there used to be joy and excitement. Was it normal to feel like this when you got engaged to someone you love? Except, she had to admit to herself, she did not love Pierre Bertrand. She liked him, yes. She admired his good taste in clothes, absolutely. She hoped he would take her to see magnificent places. But he did not stir those deep feelings inside her, feelings that ran all the way through her stomach and her heart and her mind. But did she feel ready to drop him and run away with the schoolteacher? No, she didn't, and the main reason – she told herself, but not anyone else – was that Jules Badeau had never asked her. After her birthday party three months ago, he stopped coming, as if he knew something was happening. And indeed, things happened. Her parents went to see the Bertrand family, and were received for a polite aperitif. Not dinner, but aperitif, as if they were not important enough to be invited for dinner.

They came back around eight, and brought back an autumn wind that undressed all the trees in their backyard, left them naked and trembling.

"They were looking down on us," grumbled her father and poured himself a glass of wine.

"You've had enough wine tonight, Jean," said her mother. "Don't you think?"

"Who do they think they are?" continued her father, as if he didn't hear her. "They think our family is not good enough for them? That we are peasants and they are aristocracy? They are shopkeepers, that's all. And you are the daughter of a *commercant*, too, if they don't like farmers."

"Jean, enough," begged her mother.

"What did they say, *Maman*?" asked Adele.

Her mother looked at her with her penetrating green eyes.

"They said they are fine with their son marrying you, if this is what he chooses to do," she finally said.

"Doesn't sound as if they are overly enthusiastic," said Adele.

"That doesn't matter," said her mother. "They will let their son choose who he marries, which is good enough for us. And he does want to marry you, Adele. After all, he came to talk to your father and ask him, didn't he?"

Jean Durand half laughed, half choked as he emptied his glass of wine. "He is a naïve boy, that's all he is. Not smart like the other one, but luckily for him he was born to the right family, so he won't go hungry."

"And that's important, don't you agree?" said her mother quietly, talking to her husband but not taking her eyes off Adele.

Jean Durand grunted again. "Can we eat something?" he said. "These people talk high but are not generous where food is concerned."

"Yes, Jean, I will go and get some dinner on the table," said Anne Durand quietly. "Adele, come and help me, please."

The two women walked into the kitchen, and Adele tugged on her mother's sleeve.

"*Maman*, what did they really say? Please tell me the truth. Will they accept this marriage?"

"They'll be lucky to have you as a daughter-in-law, Adele," said Anne Durand. "And they will realize this very quickly. They don't know you, that's all. My parents were a bit like that when I decided to marry your father. They didn't want me to marry a farmer, but they let me follow my heart, which was the main thing."

Adele kept quiet. *Am I following my heart?* she wondered.

They prepared the evening meal silently, and her mother served her husband and son cooked potatoes and cold chicken, keeping for Adele and herself bread from that morning and a few vegetables from the garden. The family ate silently, and her father went to bed early.

"I promised to let you do as you see fit for our children's future," he said to his wife before he went to bed, shortly after he wiped his plate clean with a dry piece of bread. "But don't ask me to like these people."

"They are good people," said Anne Durand to her husband. "And Adele will have a good life with their son. She will never go hungry and she will be able to help us in our old age."

"I can take care of us," said Jean Durand. He banged his fist on the table. "I can take care of us!" he repeated, his voice getting louder.

Adele and her mother exchanged glances.

"Of course you can, Jean," said Anne Durand. "But it's not like Adele is marrying a monster. She is marrying a handsome young man, who will one day have his own shop, or at least a part in it. And he promised to take her to Paris one day. Didn't he, Adele?"

Adele nodded. She wasn't so sure she was that keen on going to Paris anymore, not at the cost of upsetting her father so much.

"Fine then," grumbled Jean Durand. "Let her go to Paris with him, if that's what she wants."

With these words he left the table and stumbled into the bedroom, and fell asleep on his bed, fully clothed.

Twenty-Six

I sat back and stretched, having just spent three hours in front of my computer. It was near-midnight, and I was the only one awake. Many evenings I found myself in bed before the kids, exhausted from a day at work which was not that tiring, really. It was my emotional and mental state over the past few months – or to be honest with myself – for the past few years, which exhausted me. I was drained of energy, drained of enthusiasm. All I wanted to do was sleep. Now, and over the past week or so, this had suddenly changed.

Since the first regression with Tatiana, it was as if some newfound energy was flowing in my veins, some long-forgotten enthusiasm for life kept me going through the day, and allowed me to rest at night.

Was it the hypnosis? Was it just a coincidence? I wasn't one of those people who read too much into coincidences – I am pretty grounded, and I know that coincidences happen all the time. But the last week had been more than that. It was becoming eerie, as I felt that my life was turning into a jigsaw puzzle in which the pieces were being put together, one by one. Of course, I could not see the big picture, not yet. But I was beginning to sense there was one. Maybe Lauren knew something I didn't? I made a mental note to try and talk to her on Monday at the office, without admitting I'd actually been to see a hypnotherapist. That I'd actually experienced something that might have been…might have been a past-life regression. That sounded a little too 'out there' to discuss openly. But now that I thought of the past-life regression again, something inside me itched, and I felt that I really wanted to go back to this altered state of consciousness I'd experienced with Tatiana. I felt so relaxed, so non-judged, untroubled, when I was under hypnosis. Time seemed to stand still, yet an hour or two passed by as if they were ten minutes. This elasticity of time that I'd experienced was not something that I could explain away by saying it was just my imagination. It really felt as if time flowed differently under hypnosis. And it was almost addictive, I wanted to go back and experience more of it. I needed my fix.

Of course, I reasoned, I might not see Adele again. I knew that was a possibility – after all, it happened just a few days ago when I saw that strange African shaman. But I was so intrigued – by him as much as by Adele and her life story – that I did not really mind.

I got my handbag and dug out Tatiana's business card, and found the email address on it. And so I wrote her, asking for another appointment, as soon as possible.

Twenty-Seven

For many seasons his life remained mostly unchanged. From afar, he watched the children of the village grow and turn into long-limbed youths. He saw the boys becoming skilled at using spears and bows, the girls at grinding roots and tending to household chores. Some of the older girls had babies, who first rode on their backs and then crawled around in the dirt, slowly acquiring the skills necessary to walk on their two feet. All day he sat under 'his' tree, the same tree he'd been sitting under for so many years, and did not think of the future. For what was the point of thinking about the future when he knew that past, present and future meant little and this life was nothing but the figment of an existence on the other side of a veil? He was one of the fortunate ones who could see through this veil, but it also meant that what he saw on the other side attracted so much of his attention that many times things on this side looked bland, unimportant, even ridiculous.

"You never wanted a family of your own?" asked the young man who had now become his apprentice. "Does it mean that I should not have one if I want to be like you?"

"Reality is what you make it," said the older man. "My reality is such that I do not need a family here. My family is with me, my ancestors and forefathers, they always come to me when I call them."

"Yes," insisted the young man in a hesitant voice. "But I mean a family in the here and now. A woman. Maybe children who will look after you in your old age."

The older man looked into the distance. Where before there were trees he now saw only mist.

"The here and now are insignificant to me. Maybe they should mean more, otherwise I wouldn't be here. Perhaps you are right."

The young man did not press the topic any further. He was grateful that the wise man had taken him under his wing many moons ago, and was like a father to him. He did not know his own father, for no one would talk of him, certainly not his mother. When he asked her once about his father, she pretended not to understand his question, despite the fact he knew that she understood it very well. He did not even know if the man who was his father was alive or not.

His mother lived in the village, and he looked after her now that she was less strong than she used to be. As she could not speak, he was not only her protector but also her mouth. And this man, this man who had taught him everything he knew and had chosen him from amongst the many able young men who lived in the village and in the villages down the river, had also saved his life when he was an infant.

He didn't know the details of the story because his mother, in her gestures and hand-movements, could not convey them. He wanted to ask the old man, the healer, what had happened that day his mother brought him on her back, weak and very close to moving to the other side, but the healer wouldn't speak of it. He'd heard from the village women that the healer had snatched him from the clutches of Death like he had done for many others. *Sometimes he bargains with Death,* one of the village women told him. It was said that the healer gave some of his own years to Death to save a sick child. *But for some others,* said the same woman, *he could do nothing and Death just took them.*

And then one day, he accompanied his mother to see the healer again. He knew that she was very fond of the old man. She would often send him, her son, with bowls of food for the healer. He would come and lay the bowls in front of the man; he'd sometimes stay to watch him perform a ritual and would feel a strange sense of calm fall over him as he watched – as if he himself was part of the ritual. Perhaps this was why he did not feel the need to prove himself by hunting or performing other acts of bravery, like all the other boys in the village.

As he walked with his mother the distance from their hut to that of the healer, he noticed his mother nervously fiddling with something in her hand. When he looked closely, he saw it was a necklace. And he recognized it – it was the same necklace he'd seen her working on for a while now in the evenings, just before the sun had set.

They arrived at the healer's hut, and as always, they found him sitting under his tree. His mother did not make any gestures, neither did she utter one of her low, guttural sounds which she so often made when trying to express herself. She just lay the necklace on the small mat, in front of the healer. He looked at her, and picked it up. He examined it closely. It was an animal-skin necklace, from which elaborately ornamented thin stones dangled like delicate leaves from a wiry branch.

Each and every stone had a small carving on it – he could not see from his mother's side what the carvings were, but he presumed these were animals.

He watched how his mother's eyes lit up when the healer caressed the small stones, and then stretched the necklace over his head and put it around his neck without saying a word. She bowed her head and walked away, holding her son's hand. He was as tall as his mother now, and this felt awkward, but he did not pull away.

The next day the healer called for him, and asked if he would like to train with him. He said yes immediately, but the healer sent him to ask for his mother's permission.

As he ran the short distance back into the village, he felt his heart beating with unfamiliar joy.

"Mother, mother," he called as he approached their hut and then stopped. Of course, she could not hear him, how could he forget that in his excitement?

But when he went inside he found that she was not in their hut and he ran around the village, trying to find her. He finally found her sitting with a few other village women, grating roots and so he pulled her aside and tried to convey to her in words which she could not hear and in excited signs that she could understand, that the healer had offered to take him on as an apprentice. She immediately threw her arms around him and held him tight for a few moments. When she finally let go of him, he saw tears on her cheeks. These were tears of joy.

Twenty-Eight

I wasn't surprised that three weeks later, when Tatiana had an available appointment for another past-life regression, the shaman came back again. By now I was kind of expecting him, he almost felt more real than Adele and her exploits. After all, I was nearing the end of my novel now and I could connect to Adele in my head whenever I sat by my computer. I didn't know where that story came from, or how it was going to end, as it flowed from my fingertips onto the keyboard and then onto the screen in front of me like a download from the Internet. It felt as if I was writing down a distant memory more than as if I was making a story up. One way or another, Adele was a delicate and lovely, although very immature, creature. She lacked self-confidence and thought she could manipulate everyone around her to get what she wanted. I couldn't say that I liked her that much, but I certainly felt for her; I had an emotional stake in what was going to happen to her. And as I did not yet know what the end of my story would be, I was keen to get to the end of my novel and find out.

Meanwhile, everyday life became somewhat calmer, more pleasant, as if I'd found a comfortable path to walk on. I was back at my desk, enthusiastically reading mostly great books and pitching them to foreign publishers, whom I'd been working with for the past fifteen years. I had a business-trip to Paris coming up, and I was excited about going back to the city of my birth, which I'd visited a handful of times since I'd left it at the age of thirteen. I hoped Don could look after the kids for a week – it wasn't too much to ask of him, was it?

But the most surprising thing for me was the change I'd noticed in Jen over the past three weeks. She asked to go and train at the fencing club twice a week after school, and I saw no problem with that, if she could manage all her homework, too.

She started talking about buying equipment, which I didn't think we could afford right then.

"See if you really want to continue, Jen," I said when she came back all bright-eyed from her first bout.

"Of course I do, Mom," she reprimanded me. "It's so awesome. It's like...nothing else I've done before."

"And Gabriel?" I asked. "How does he fit into all of this?"

"He's there," she said, a mischievous smile on her lips. "I took the subway with him today, from school to the club."

"Hmm," I said. "So it worked."

She smiled.

"You know, Mom," she then said. "I started this to be able to connect to Gabriel, but now I can actually see what he is so passionate about. I love it. I can't wait until I'm good enough to do competitions. In fact, I'd love to go and watch one this weekend...a competition Gabriel is in... Can I?"

I could not see why not – the club apparently had arranged transportation for all the fencers and their supporters – I was just happy my daughter suddenly looked all bright-eyed. Tom was his usual distracted self, absorbed in his schoolwork and friends. There was even a girl in his life now; I overheard some conversations he'd had on his phone while he was coming in or leaving the house – but he didn't let me in on the details.

Tom was the kind of guy that could always find the positive in any situation – or rather, the kind of guy that did not notice the negative. I knew he'd do well in life, while Jen – she was more like me. She always put on a tough exterior, but behind it, she was sensitive and emotional.

A positive wind had blown into our lives – and although I could feel the pleasant breeze, I could not explain it.

I was not even bothered by Don and his quirks, and when he cancelled yet another weekend with the kids only three weeks after he'd gone to that party Upstate New York, I just said – fine. We'd be busy anyway; Jen had asked whether she could attend a fencing competition.

"A what?" he said, his voice on the other end of the line distant and distracted.

"A fencing competition," I repeated.

"What's that?"

"Fencing? It's a sport," I said knowingly. "An Olympic sport." I heard him snorting.

"I know that," he then said. "Since when is Jen fencing?"

"Don't you ever talk to your daughter?"

I could not hold it in much longer.

"She started a month ago, and it's become this huge thing in her life. She trains twice a week. And now she wants to try to compete, so if you can't take them this weekend, then I'll go with her to her first competition. She'll be disappointed you're too busy to see her, but she'll be happy to know that she can go to this competition."

He ignored my comment about being too busy.

"Oh," he said. "Ok then. Tell them I'll get them the following weekend, if that's ok?"

"That's ok," I said. I didn't want to ask him to help foot the bill for the fencing equipment I was about to buy for Jen: a fencing mask, a fencing glove and an electric saber. I figured that could wait until I saw him in ten days or so.

Instead, I just sat in front of my computer again, and let the frustration Don made me feel evaporate, as words started flowing effortlessly onto my keyboard.

Twenty-Nine

Anne Durand made the dress for her daughter's post-wedding reception from the blue-gray fabric. She sewed it into a flowing gown that just touched the floor with sleeves that covered Adele's wrists, even though the wedding would take place on a warm day in June, a month short of Adele's nineteenth birthday.

"It is more elegant this way, and you will look *magnifique* in it," said her mother, holding it close to Adele's body. "This color does suit you. And now you will have no shortage of dresses, that's for certain."

Adele smiled at her mother. She felt happy, most days. Every now and again she had doubts that were eating at her, doubts about the wedding, about becoming a wife, about becoming Pierre Bertrand's wife. She only shared them with her mother once.

"It's normal," said Anne Durand. "Everyone has doubts before they get married; it is a big change in life."

"Are you crazy?" said her friend Eugénie when she confided in her that she was having these doubts. "I'll marry him if you don't."

Adele laughed, but this didn't make her feel any better. She realized of course that Pierre Bertrand was a good catch, and if she didn't hurry up and marry him herself, she would, most definitely, lose him to someone else.

And so, the wedding was planned and the groom's family said they would assume the cost of the reception, which was to take place at the Bertrand's large family home in Gex, not far from the church.

"I hope they will give the guests some real food," muttered

Adele's father when he heard that it was his in-law's specific request to organize the meal themselves and decide what would be served without consulting the Durands. After all, they would be paying for it.

They also limited the Durands' guests to thirty, which did not go down well in the village.

"Of course, you and Monsieur Montague are invited," said Anne Durand to her neighbor. "But I don't quite know how to make the list for the other guests. Only my side of the family, my brother and two sisters and their families, bring us up to twenty. They will all come from Lyon, so they will have to stay with us. And of course, we need to invite Jean's family and distant relatives. I don't know what to do."

"Offer to pay for some of the costs," suggested Madame Montague.

"I don't want to offend them and start on the wrong foot," said Anne Durand. "We will always be the poor relations anyway, so we might as well get used to it from the beginning."

As the big day approached, Adele saw Pierre Bertrand more and more often – they were now allowed to take walks together without anyone else accompanying them – and she started getting used to him. He showed up every weekend, driven by carriage from Gex, with the driver waiting outside the Durand house while Monsieur Bertrand was having his tea with the family, always followed by a short walk with Adele on days it was not raining.

Jean Durand often took some food and drink out to the driver and had a chat with him. It seemed to Adele that her father felt he had more in common with the driver than with his future son-in-law, but she also noticed he made an effort to talk to Pierre, was never rude to him and was careful not to get drunk in his presence.

Two weeks before the wedding Adele finally confided in Pierre that the number of guests allocated to her family by his own was somewhat tight and he surprised her by sending a note with the driver that very night, saying that he had got his parents to raise the number to fifty, if she could find twenty people to invite at such short notice.

Madame Durand quickly went out the next morning and invited three more families from the village, explaining that there had been a misunderstanding and of course they'd been on the list of invitees all along.

"See, he is a generous man, even if his parents aren't," she said to her husband Jean.

"Show me the tree and I will tell you about the apple," he answered.

"Don't be so negative," she said. "Can't you see how happy our daughter is?"

"Actually, I can't," he replied.

"Well, she would be," concluded his wife.

After the church service everyone walked to the Bertrand house, led by the bride and the groom in a decorated carriage pulled by two handsome dark horses. Adele felt dizzy, as if she was in a dream. She sat next to a man she hardly knew, but who was now holding her hand and smiling at her. A man who was handsome and well respected and had good prospects. A man whom she would, from now on, call 'husband'. So why was she feeling as if she was sitting next to a stranger?

She smiled back at Pierre Bertrand.

"Madame Bertrand," he said to her and squeezed her hand. "Is everything all right?"

She nodded. "Yes, of course. I look forward to the reception party, and to changing into my comfortable new dress. This dress is wonderful but I don't think I can dance in it!"

Her wedding dress, made of ivory layers of dupioni silk

brought especially from Paris, was stunning. Her mother-in-law had had it made for her, for she would not be happy for her son to marry someone wearing an ordinary wedding dress.

Adele was grateful and appreciative of this new dress, although she knew she would not wear it more than once in her entire life and it did seem somewhat wasteful. She had never touched anything so fine before, but the boned bodice restricted her movements and Adele, who was used to running around freely in comfortable and practical attire suddenly felt like a prisoner in her extravagant dress.

This is what ladies and princesses must feel like, she thought to herself. *That's why they take such tiny steps and don't make any large gestures wearing dresses like this one. It is simply impossible.*

She loved her wedding dress but looked forward to being able to get out of it and wear the comfortable, pretty dress her mother had made for her out of the blue-gray fabric. Her mother used the same pattern she had used for the yellow dress, except the sleeves were longer, and covered her wrists. The waist of her new dress had hand-embroidered flowers, giving it the appearance of luxury and elegance. Her mother was a gifted seamstress, no doubt.

Adele knew that her mother was initially taken aback by the determination of the Bertrands to control each and every detail of the ceremony, even the wedding dress. But Madame Durand was relieved when she learned that they had no specific plans for the reception dress, she told Adele as much. And she took the folded fabric from the top shelf of the cupboard in Adele's room and spent many afternoons and evenings putting together the most fabulous dress she could create.

"I love this dress but I can't really move much in it," Adele told Pierre again as the carriage was about to stop in front of his parents' home. She couldn't think of another topic of conversation, and wanted to say something, anything. The silence between them bothered her.

"I look forward to changing into the dress my mother made out of the fabulous fabric you sent me for my birthday."

Pierre seemed distracted for a moment as he looked back at the dozens of people behind them, all waiting for the bride and groom to descend from the carriage, so they could all enter his parents' large home for an afternoon of festivities.

"Sorry, *ma cherie*? What did you say?"

"Oh, nothing important. Just that I look forward to wearing the fabulous dress my mother made out of the blue-gray fabric you gave me for my birthday. I don't believe I ever even thanked you for it. It must have cost a fortune."

Pierre looked at her with his large hazel eyes. "I didn't give you any fabric for your birthday," he said. "You are surely confused. But I look forward to seeing you in that fabulous dress nonetheless. I am sure you'll look beautiful in it, Madame Bertrand."

Thirty

The strips, or pistes as Jen now referred to them, looked like blue magic carpets rolled at the feet of alien creatures dressed in sparkling white and metal silver. I accompanied Jen into the large gymnasium, paid her competition fee and then found a seat on the bleachers.

I searched for Jen but I couldn't see her – she must have gone back to the changing-rooms, or to attend a briefing by one of the coaches.

My heart skipped a beat when I suddenly noticed Noah in the distance, talking to one of his young students. He bent down to speak to a boy, maybe twelve or thirteen years old. Even from a distance I could tell the boy was nervous, preparing for a bout. I had never watched a fencing competition before, and did not know what to expect, but as soon as the referee called *en garde* and then *prets* and *allez* the two boys bolted towards each other, pointing their sabers as one advanced and the other backed away in small but quick steps. I only knew these were sabers because Jen had explained that this would be a saber competition, but that there were two other fencing arms – foil and epee – the latter was not practiced at her club.

Noah did not notice my presence, or if he did, he did not acknowledge it. I couldn't help but wonder what the story was – he made this effort to trace me down, call me, meet me – and then just acted as if I didn't exist.

True, as a fencing coach he was surrounded by many beautiful young women, but he didn't seem to be that kind of guy who'd be chasing young girls – for goodness sake, he was in his mid-forties, like me. He didn't seem to be married – I admitted to myself now that I did look for a wedding ring on his finger when we met in the café – and couldn't see one. He had not mentioned a wife or children, but maybe he had a girlfriend. And why wouldn't he? He was good-looking, especially when he wore all black. He was smart, and had a great job – but – of course, there was the slightly dysfunctional aspect of his personality that was becoming more and more obvious to me. I knew little about Asperger's syndrome, but of course, it appeared in books, movies, even the newspapers recently. It was a condition on the autism spectrum, although a usually mild form of autism that came with higher-than-average intelligence and some social dysfunctions that were not necessarily crippling, but they could be if not given enough attention as the child grew up.

But Noah – he seemed to have found his place within society, doing something he loved. I was intrigued by his specific memories of the teenage me – was he now disappointed by the middle-aged me, which is why he'd decided to ignore me, or was it his 'condition' that made him seem so distant, so uncommunicative?

The loudspeaker called out a list of names, and Jennifer Rothman was one of them. Those fencers were called to strip three, and I saw my daughter advancing towards the blue strip in her white fencing clothes and silver jacket.

"I know I won't be doing well in this competition," she had said earlier. "But Sergey said it would be good for me to gain some experience, just see what it's like to be out there on the strip, in a real competition".

I just hoped she wouldn't get hurt.

"Hello, Amelia."

The voice from behind surprised me. I had just seen Noah down there, busy with his students. How did he even see me? It was true that the bleachers were not completely full; a few dozen families sat there, waiting to watch the competition. These were nothing like the packed bleachers in many other sports events. I guess he must have known I'd come and accompany Jen.

"Hi," I said, surprised to feel myself blushing. "How are you?"

"Good. Saber is my favorite weapon," he said, as if answering a different question all together. "That's why I specialized in it. There's more strategy to it. It's a little like chess, where you have to understand your opponent's weak spot and play on it. There are many kinds of attacks you can use, and it depends on your opponent's strategy and on the tactic you use to contradict it. The best strategy would not work if not matched to your opponent's."

"Oh," I said. "Ok."

There was an awkward short silence, as if Noah realized he hadn't said quite the right thing.

"Right," he said. "Got to go back down there. I just wanted to say hello."

"Hello," I said, realizing that it was now me who had just said the wrong thing. What was happening here? It was as if we were talking on a bad telephone line, not quite getting each other's messages.

"See you later," he said as he climbed back up the bleachers to take the stairs down into the gymnasium.

"Yes," I said. "See you later."

The competition lasted just over three hours, and I spent some of it watching my daughter fence and lose bitterly, although quite graciously. I spent a part of those three hours daydreaming, thinking about how my novel should end, and some of the time I spent reading the Sunday edition of the *New York Times*. In the cultural section there was a special feature dedicated to France, with a focus on rural destinations. I was looking forward to my business-trip to Paris and had no intention of visiting rural France, but then something caught my eye. It was a small article about the Pays de Gex, in southeast France.

The Pays de Gex is an historical region in the northeast of the department of Ain, the article said. It became part of France in

1061, and before that changed hands several times between the states of Savoie, Barnoie and Geneva. Voltaire moved there in 1754, when he escaped from Paris following some scandals his writing and opinions caused, and he reached Ferney, right on the Swiss border, where he built a chateau, known today as the chateau of Ferney-Voltaire. It was a very short distance from Geneva in Switzerland, it said, so Voltaire knew he could easily escape to the second chateau he had acquired in the city of Calvin. I didn't know much about Geneva or about Calvin, but the article went on to describe the many tourist attractions the area had to offer and how beautiful it was.

Something about this piece of travel writing gripped me, as if I was reading a thriller. I was so engrossed by it that I even missed one of Jen's matches, but it was another one she lost so I didn't feel too bad.

In fact, I suddenly felt exhilarated, as if someone had just handed me the key to finishing my novel. Gex. I remembered the name of the place – from my hypnosis session, and then from my own writing – even though I didn't know that it actually existed until this very moment. I googled it on my Blackberry, and sure enough, it came up as a name of a town in southeast France, very close to Switzerland.

I didn't know what this all meant, but I just knew I wanted to visit this place and see if it had any resonance for me, for Adele's story. How far was it from Paris? A quick check on my phone showed it was about 300 miles, or a three-hour train-ride from Paris. Should I? Could I? I decided to follow the overwhelming gut-feeling I had about visiting this place. In fact, I felt as if I had no choice – it was such a strong sensation that it took hold of me as if I had no will of my own. I *needed* to visit this place. *This will help me understand more about Adele's world, it will be research, not some craziness destined to satisfy my sudden and illogical fascination with past lives*, I said to myself.

Thirty-One

The white men stood in a clearing in the center of the village and a circle of children gathered around them, tagging at their clothes and running their little fingers on the pale skin of their hands. A little boy, no older than three or four years old, grabbed one of the strangers' fingers and would not let go. He kept trying to scrape the pale skin off the hand, to see if beneath the white there would be a layer of dark skin. He was very disappointed when there wasn't. He then carefully touched the man's clothes, as if afraid they were going to sting him. The feel of the unfamiliar, soft fabric made him laugh, his perfect white little teeth gleaming in the sunlight.

"He is not back," said one of the village elders. The translator translated to the foreign men standing beside him.

They looked at each other and frowned. The small crowed around them quieted into an uncomfortable, fragile silence that was louder than the shrieks of the monkeys that could be heard from afar.

"Do you know when he will return?" asked the bearded man, his voice quivering into a menacing vibration.

The village elders looked at each other, none of them wanting to be the one talking back to the tall, bearded man.

"He will be back when the forefathers have spoken, maybe in a moon or two," one of them finally said, looking at the translator, who immediately conveyed his words to the Portuguese man.

Again there was silence.

Then some rapid words were exchanged among the men in their guttural language and a message was barked at the translator. He hesitated before translating.

"They require ten strong young men to come with them," he finally said, avoiding the elders' eyes. "They want them now."

The elders said nothing. A strong shift in the energy was felt, as if the red earth suddenly became alive with tension. A slight breeze rustled the leaves of the nearby trees, but the village men remained silent, as if letting the sounds of the jungle speak in their stead.

The foreigners looked around them uncomfortably, searching for hidden natives, perhaps warriors, they suspected might be watching them from afar, but they could see none.

This loud silence lasted a few moments, when the sound of faraway thunder rolled in from the west. It was a muffled sound, filled with the energy of the earth and accompanied by pregnant, gray clouds rolling in slowly above their heads. The Portuguese men looked at each other, realizing that a sudden rainstorm in the jungle would put them at an immediate disadvantage.

"Strange to have a thunderstorm on such a clear day," commented one of the men.

The elders looked at each other.

"Perhaps these are the forefathers, making their presence known," said one of them. The translator kept quiet.

"We've come to take ten young men with us," tried the bearded man again. "We will give them food and clothes in return. Even jewelry."

The translator remained silent.

"Tell them," said the bearded man. "Tell them to bring ten men."

Suddenly, from behind them, the soft sound of bare feet on red earth was heard and when they turned they could see behind them not ten young men, but twenty or twenty-five of them, their faces smeared with red paint. Each of them held a spear, and most of those spears were now pointed at the Portuguese men.

The faraway thunder rolled again, and the wind picked up.

"I think we'd better leave now," said one of the Portuguese

men.

"They know the jungle much better than us," muttered another.

"Let's get out of here. We can always come back tomorrow," added the first.

The bearded man hesitated for a moment or two.

"Tell them we'll be back tomorrow for the men," he barked at the translator, who immediately conveyed the message to the elders.

"The ancestors cannot be rushed, you know that," said one of the elders stubbornly.

The translator just shrugged in response, and the foreign men gathered their affairs and returned to their boats on the river, looking behind them at the group of armed youths who followed them from a short distance. The bearded man was the last to turn and leave, his long firearm swinging on his wide back.

Thirty-Two

It was the first time I dreamt of the shaman. As if Adele, who was now married to the wrong man, decided to play games with me and disappear. Where was she? What happened to her? I needed to know, in order to be able to finish my novel. I also wanted to know because it felt as if I had some kind of stake in what happened to her.

So why were the shaman and his world populating my dreams now? It was truly disturbing, because while I could identify with Adele and her story on some level, I could not understand how this shaman was connected to me – he was such a strange character, so different from everyone I'd ever known or imagined. He was fascinating, he was kind and had an aura of wisdom about him, but he was so lonely, so sad, he didn't fit in. Why was I dreaming about him now?

I sat in front of my computer every single evening, five evenings in a row, trying to finish Adele's story. But nothing came to me. Just as suddenly as the story started flowing after my first hypnosis session with Tatiana, it had now stopped. I felt blocked – it wasn't even writer's block, it was more like some kind of information blockage. I knew I had this information somewhere in the back of my mind, but I could not access it. I thought of going back to Tatiana for another session, but by now my hypnotherapy was starting to get expensive. After paying for Jen's fencing lessons and equipment, I had to be careful with my own expenses. Jen's fencing or my hypnotherapy sessions is what it came down to, and I didn't have to think for long to decide which one it would be.

I decided to talk to Don when he came to pick up the children the following Friday – ask him to help pay for Jen's fencing, and ask him to have them for two weeks, so I could extend my business trip to France and turn it into a research trip. It wouldn't be much more costly than a few more sessions with Tatiana, I justified it to myself. The flight would be paid for anyway as a business expense.

Don wasn't on the same wavelength.

"Two weeks?" he asked, running his fingers through his thinning black hair. I noticed he'd dyed it, something he never did when we were together. It was I who started to dye my hair even before I turned thirty, because white hair was starting to peek through my chestnut curls, especially at the temples.

"That's a long time for a business trip to Paris," he added as an afterthought, which wasn't an afterthought at all. I knew how his mind worked – he was trying to get more information.

"I am staying on to do some research," I said.

"Research?"

"Yes, for my novel. Some of it is set in France."

"Oh, your novel," he said, as if he had a bite of sour fruit.

"Yes, my novel," I said. "It's nearly done."

"Congratulations," he said. "I've been hearing about it for years."

I overcame my urge to insult him, perhaps mention some of the things I've had to put up with for years because of him. I really did need his help with the kids this time.

"Well," I said, "it's nearly done now. I just need to get some details, so I'll be continuing to the southeast of France for a few days after Paris. Is that a problem?"

"No," he said. "Why would it be a problem?"

"Good," I said. "Otherwise I can ask my mom to come and look after them."

I knew my mom probably wouldn't be able to come and look after the kids for two weeks – her health was not great these days, and she was happy with the warm Florida climate and her very structured week, full of social activities. But I also knew how much Don disliked her, and hoped this would get rid of any hesitation, if he had any.

"No, it's ok, I can do it," he said, sounding more convinced than he had just two minutes before.

"Great," I said. "Thanks."

I considered talking to him about money for Jen's fencing but decided to postpone it to the end of the weekend, when he brought the kids back. I hoped he'd hear from Jen directly and see her excitement about fencing. I hoped she'd also mention the steep cost of the lessons and the equipment. Perhaps he would then offer to pay for some of it without my having to ask him. True, he could be cynical and aloof, uninterested and distant toward me, but he did love his children, and he certainly wasn't a bad guy. After all, I did marry him, and that probably served a learning purpose in my life. By now I had no doubt that our journeys often happen in mysterious ways, and I could hardly wait to find out more about mine.

Thirty-Three

He spent a day and a night in the jungle and they did not come until the afternoon of the second day. This was unusual, for when he needed their advice he would call upon them and they would be there, just like that. Not physically, of course, but they would be present in his mind, their voices loud and clear, often answering his questions before he could pose them.

But this occasion felt bigger, more powerful, as if something substantial was about to change.

After he left the village he walked for a while, until he found the makeshift hut he had built himself, deep in the forest, many years back. He would go there every time he wanted to get away from the village, from people, from distractions. There was not much in there but a small woven mat and a cover to keep him warm at night, but that cover was damp now. He would need to light a fire to keep the animals away at night, but he wouldn't need any food because he planned to fast until the forefathers gave him the answers. He knew that it would help to keep his mind clear and focused. Food tended to make him sleepy.

That first night he had waited in vain. No matter how much he tried to focus and how much he chanted, his mind had stayed crystal clear but present, none of the mist that came with the contact from The Other Side. At night he fell asleep despite the cold and the howling and rustling of the animals around. In fact, he slept so well he could not even remember his dreams, which was also unusual. Did he get any messages at night, anything he could not remember? He pushed that thought away, for he did not believe this was possible.

And then, they were there. After fasting a day and a night, his body entered a state of being in which he was no longer hungry. His mind was sharp and focused, even if his head was spinning.

When they finally came, their answer was clear. He did not even have to ask the question, to know for certain that the white men, arrogant and intrusive, were not to be trusted.

"*Their intentions are not pure*," said the voice in his head. "*Send them away.*"

"And what of the village men they wish to take with them?" he asked, and he could feel a cloud of dust rising, a breeze in a place so deep in the jungle no breeze could normally be felt, and he knew the answer.

Then he could hear the faraway rolling of thunder and the trees above his head started speaking in tongues, whispering and grunting and accompanying the crash of thunder and the howling of the wind.

All he could do then was repeat what he had heard, and so he howled and he whispered and he called out to the ancestors for help, for he knew that without their help, all might be lost by the time he made it back to the village.

When he came out of his altered state he felt exhausted at first, but then a surge of energy washed over him and he got onto his feet and started striding back to the village as if chased by a pack of wild dogs. He knew only one thing for certain – he had to stop the young village men from going along with the pale people, from falling into the trap of their shiny beads and peculiar long spears that could hunt an animal from afar.

As he walked back towards the village he was encountered by a strange silence and the thin grin of a moon that had no reflection, not even in the river. He absent-mindedly touched the stones around his neck; the necklace given to him by the deaf-dumb woman filled him with a warm sensation, a feeling of being appreciated, cared for. It made him smile. But then he remembered the mission ahead and walked into the village itself, something he'd rarely done. He banged his cane against the stump of the baobab around which the huts were built in a circle. He remembered the day this giant tree was cut down, when he was still a child. It was a rainy day and all the men in the village prepared for the big job. The boys were told they would be allowed to help, not in the cutting down of the tree, but once the men had managed to release the spirit of the tree and cut it down, the boys could then help carry it away and store the wood for fire.

The village women cooked all day for the feast which was planned for that night, but the tree did not come down that night for it had a stubborn spirit, and the celebration had to be postponed by several days.

His grandfather, who was the village sorcerer and healer, walked around the voluminous, bulbous trunk and chanted for hours, asking the spirit of the tree to leave. He apologized for having to cut it down, but it had a disease which made it turn all black and the ancestors said it had to go.

It was the tree that had always been the center of the village; it was around this tree that first ten, then twenty, then more huts were put up. And it was around this tree that the life of the village was to continue evolving, but without the thick, twisted branches looming over the villagers' heads.

"It has to be cut down," said the ancestors to his grandfather, but when the village men did try to cut it down, the tree spewed out dark water at them, like sick blood.

The village kids shrieked when the brown water splashed out of the tree and the men it had hit ran to the river, to wash it off, for fear it might curse them.

"It is the spirit of the tree that does not want to leave," explained his grandfather, and he – just a small boy – wanted to help and explain to this spirit that by releasing it from the sick tree, they were actually helping it go back to The Source of

Things and get a new life. He did not know quite how to convince the stubborn spirit, but two moons later, when the tree finally came down and the whole village gathered around a big fire that was set to celebrate the parting with the cut-down trunk, he knew that the spirit was appeased.

And now, standing by this stump of the tree that carried so much significance for him, so many memories, he felt confused and alarmed. What had happened in the time he was away? Did the white men come back? And did they take anyone with them?

He thumped the stump with his cane again, a rhythmic and measured beat. Just a few short moments later, a few men emerged from their huts, gathering by the baobab stump under the thin moon.

"They've gone away but they will be back," said one of the elders, fastening a cover around his naked shoulders.

"They wanted to take some young men away, but we didn't let them," said another.

"It is the forefathers who did not let them; they let the thunder loose and the men ran away," clarified a third.

The healer just looked at them without saying a word.

"So what do we do, Uncle?" one of the men asked him. "Can you help us?"

The healer just stared ahead, unable to convey to them the terror that he felt inside, the hesitation and apprehension that took over him when he realized that to help his people he would have to cross a line, a line he had been careful not to cross during his entire lifetime. To help his people he would have to cross, the forefathers had told him, the invisible line between a healer and a sorcerer.

Thirty-Four

Adele's sudden disappearance was a mystery and I could not understand why she had been replaced by this strange shaman.

Jen and Tom were gone all weekend, and I hoped they were having a nice time with Don. The initial bitterness I felt when I learned they would be spending every second weekend with him and skinny Claudette had been replaced by a longing for sitting by my keyboard, uninterrupted, for hours on end.

I wanted to finish my novel, I wanted to get to the end of Adele's story, but instead, this African tale of magic and sorcery had emerged from somewhere in the depth of my mind, triggered by my hypnosis sessions. I now ached for the company of this strange imaginary man, this shaman – was he connected to Adele somehow? The writer in me said *yes*. The editor in me asked, *how*?

The only way to find out was to let his story develop, and as I couldn't afford any more sessions with Tatiana in the foreseeable future, the cheaper alternative was to spend hours on end in front of my computer, fueled by coffee and the occasional sandwich that I managed to fix without too much effort, and write.

Saturday passed by as if it were a dream, and when I paid attention to the clock on the top right of my computer screen that showed eight p.m., I was startled. I'd been sitting without even a washroom break for nearly seven hours. And they felt like twenty minutes. *It's almost like the shaman's altered state of consciousness*, I thought.

I found something similar between the state of consciousness of writing and that of being under hypnosis – the same sense of elasticity of time. Time flowed as if there were no hours or minutes or seconds, just an endless stream of moments, which had no beginning or end until something interrupted me.

And something did, just after eight p.m. It was the phone again.

As I picked it up I had a feeling in the pit of my stomach, a hope mixed with some apprehension, of whose voice I might hear on the other end.

Then there was a brief moment of silence, as if someone on the other end was trying to make up his or her mind whether to hang up or not.

"Hello," I said. "Who's there?"

"Hi," I heard the voice on the other end, which I immediately recognized. "I…I hope I am not disturbing you, it's just that…"

"No problem at all, Noah," I said. "How are you?"

This seemed to cheer him up.

"Oh, good," he said. "I had a very busy week and I meant to call you sooner and say that I think your daughter did really well on that bout last weekend although I know it wasn't easy for her. But it's good to get bout experience."

"Sure," I said. And I waited. Surely he didn't call me just for that on a Saturday night?

"Ok," he said. "Well, I also wanted to ask…"

Then another moment of silence. Should I try to make it easier for him? Should I take the risk of making a fool of myself?

"If I wanted to go out for a drink?" I said. The words escaped my mouth before I could stop them.

I could hear him sighing with relief.

"Yes," he said, "would you like to?"

I was the one sighing with relief now – that he didn't just want to ask me something else about fencing.

"When?"

"Is…is now too late?"

"Now, as in…now?"

I really didn't know whether this was a good idea. So he did have some kind of interest in me, whether nostalgic or romantic

I really could not tell – because he didn't express his feelings in a way that I could understand. Or was he just playing some kind of game with me?

The silence was getting awkward and I felt a need to fill it. "I'm working on my novel, not sure it's a good idea to stop now, as I'm on the go."

"You're writing a novel?"

"Yeah."

"What is it about?"

How do I tell him? Do I know myself?

"It's about... I suppose it's about intertwined lives."

"What does that mean?"

"Well, it's like when we hadn't seen each other for twenty-something years and suddenly our paths cross, and perhaps there's a reason for it that we don't understand. Only it's more complex than that."

"Right," he said. "I think I get it. It's like when things happen for a reason, and you can feel it even if you don't believe in destiny or whatever you want to call it, but you can still feel it."

"Right," I said. "I think they call it karma. But destiny's a good word for it, too."

We continued speaking for a while, mostly about intertwined lives, but also about our past, and our present.

I learned that he was divorced, with his ex-wife and daughter still living in San Francisco.

"That's actually the reason I moved to New York City," he said. "This whole divorce thing was really hard for me. When I got this job, it was a lifeline. I didn't hesitate for a moment."

It was surprising to feel a small explosion of joy when I learnt that he was single. I hadn't thought I was particularly fond of him – at least, not at first. But now I felt differently – I felt as if I'd definitely give him a chance, if he asked for one.

If he only took the initiative, if he asked me out again...then maybe I would accept.

The next time I looked at the top-right corner of my computer screen, it was ten p.m. We'd been speaking for two hours.

"I normally hate talking on the phone," he said. "But with you it's different."

"Why do you hate talking on the phone?"

"It's hard, when I don't see people's faces, I have to take their words at face value. And from experience I know that people don't actually mean what they say."

I pondered on that for a moment. *I suppose he's right*, I thought.

"Guess it's too late to go out now," I said, and I could sense him smiling at the other end, although I couldn't remember ever actually seeing him smile – he was more the serious, strong type. "I better go back to my novel. Or to sleep."

"Right," he said. "Good luck with that."

"Thanks," I said before I realized he'd unceremoniously hung up on me.

Thirty-Five

"They are here! They are here!"

The call spread through the village like fire in the thatched roof of a hut.

The village women gathered their children and ran into the forest, especially careful not to leave behind the older boys.

The men gathered silently and solemnly around the baobab stump. Someone went to fetch the healer. He walked slowly down the path from his hut at the outskirts of the village, shuffling his feet, arriving at the same time as the group of white men. He looked right through them, standing with his back to the tree, as if gathering strength from it.

The air stood still, the silence unnatural for this mid-morning hour. Even the birds and the families of monkeys that usually chirruped and chattered throughout the day were nowhere to be seen or heard.

The Portuguese man spoke first.

"We are back," said the bearded man. "We are here to trade peacefully."

As he spoke, he caressed the stock of his rifle.

The village men remained silent, their gazes focused on the healer.

"So who do we talk to?" asked another white man, tall and bony. The translator conveyed the Portuguese jumble-of-words to the village men. And still, they remained silent.

"We now want twenty young men to come with us," said the bearded man.

The silence was overwhelming.

The healer finally spoke.

"You cannot take our young men," he said. "The forefathers

have spoken."

The translator hesitated, but then conveyed the message.

"They will come with us," said the bearded man. "Now."

"We need them here in the village. They will not go with you," said the healer.

"We will pay you for them," said the bearded man. He started taking something out of his large leather pouch, but the healer stopped him with one motion of his palm.

"Tell him," he turned to the translator, "that we do not need what they want to give us. We have everything we need and they should just go back to where they came from."

The translator spoke, and the Portuguese men looked at each other.

The standoff lasted a few moments.

"We are not asking, we are telling you that these men will come with us, but we prefer that they come willingly," said the bearded man.

Another moment of silence followed.

Suddenly, as if conducted by an invisible hand, the monkeys started screeching – not their everyday chatter, the aaacchhh and oooccchhh and their usual cackle barks, but high-pitched, desperate sounds that were painful to the ear and carried a sound of longing and of pain, of fear, of hopelessness. The Portuguese men, unaccustomed to these jungle sounds, were startled. The village men, sensing something was simply not right, huddled together.

The healer looked the bearded man straight in the eye. "Take your men and leave," he said. The translator stuttered as he translated the angry words.

One of the white men jumped back and called out in fear as a murky-black and shiny-green snake dropped out of a tree and started crawling towards him, leaving a thin trail in the red earth.

The village elders looked at each other, puzzled, for they had never seen a tree snake behave in that manner before. These tree snakes normally used their strength to hang from high branches, their magnificent green color mingling with the leaves. They patiently and passively awaited an opportunity to snatch their pray – a bird or a small mammal. They were shy, but lethal predators, with venom that could make a grown man bleed to death from every orifice within one moon.

The group of Portuguese men backed away from the baobab stump, the tree snake crawling towards them as if possessed; the thin and silent natives staring at them with charcoal eyes. And that healer, that medicine-man, that sorcerer, standing there in his loin cloth, clutching his wooden stick, another poisonous black-and-green snake curling at his feet as if it were a harmless pet, stared at them with eyes that were calm and confident, like the jungle before a storm.

"We will be back," shouted the bearded man, waving his rifle at them. "We'll be back and you'll regret this."

The translator didn't bother to translate the ominous words as the group of white men headed back to their boats on the river.

Thirty-Six

I woke up with a start. It was now Sunday, almost midday. I had not only slept through the night, but I had slept nearly ten hours. My sleep was so deep, as if it were drug induced. I searched through my mind – did I drink? Had I taken a sleeping pill? I was certain I'd done neither.

After my conversation with Noah the night before, I wrote a little more of my novel, but it was not going anywhere so I walked around the empty apartment, my steps echoing loudly in my own ears. And then I went to bed, thinking about everything – my novel, Adele, the shaman, and my conversation with Noah. Then, I found myself wishing he'd call again.

I knew the kids would not be back until early evening, and I wondered what to do on my own, on such a beautiful Sunday. The sun was now high up in the sky and as I showered, dressed and made myself some scrambled eggs for brunch, I started wondering – what if?

What if I showed up at the club and bumped into Noah. What if I called him there, as I had no other number for him – to see if he was working this Sunday, like the previous month when we'd met for coffee. What if I asked him if he wanted to have coffee later today. What if he'd walk out on me again. What if he didn't and things went further between us. What if they didn't?

I decided not to take the risk. After all, I had just found a space in which I was comfortable with myself, with my life. Did I need any more turbulence? Surely not.

Was I looking for love? Not really. I was looking for accomplishment, I wanted to finish my novel, perhaps have it published. In my line of work I had enough contacts to help with that – if my writing was good enough and if I ever managed to finish the damn thing. And for that, I needed to go to France, to look for more hints about what Adele's life could mean – on what it could mean in my own life.

I researched a little on the Internet the area of Gex in southeast France, and I learned another interesting fact: CERN, the European Organization for Nuclear Research was based there, not far from Geneva. They had a museum, which was open to visitors, and I wrote down the opening days and hours. Perhaps I could visit it if I had time.

I found out on Wikipedia that, historically, that area had changed hands several times and had finally been declared to be part of France in the Lyon treaty of 1601. France was a Roman Catholic state back then, and until the separation of the church and the state in 1905 most teachers were clergymen, although the French Revolution that started in 1789 had planted the seeds for the secularism of France that would follow just over a century later. I found all this fascinating. So was the schoolteacher in my dreams, and in my novel, a clergyman? Was that why he was not fond of drinking? And if he was a clergyman, a Roman Catholic one at that, how could he marry Adele, even if she had not chosen to marry someone else? Was he not part of the church? If so, he must have been a forward thinker, someone in the avant-garde of his times. It was all a mixture of facts that didn't make sense to me – they didn't add up to my experience and to the story I was determined to finish, and this strengthened my resolution to take that trip to the Pays de Gex, to see what part of my story was based on fact, and which part of it was based on pure, made-up fantasy. It was only three weeks away – I could surely wait that long, and perhaps then I would have some answers.

Then I closed the Google window, thought of trying to write some more about Adele, but it didn't feel like the right moment. There was too much information missing. So I closed my eyes in some sort of improvised meditation, and invited the shaman back. And he came.

Thirty-Seven

The men advanced in their wooden boats, rowing slowly along the narrow river. The silence around them still felt unnatural, unnerving. They did not exchange any words as the four African rowers swept the water with their oars in rhythmic moves.

The bearded man looked around in silence, his eyes narrowing, as if searching for something among the thick greenery on the riverbanks.

"What?" asked the man sitting next to him. "Do you think they are following us?"

The bearded man shook his head. "I know they are up to something," he said. "I just don't know what it is."

A bloodcurdling scream pierced the rhythmic swishing of the oars and made the men in the boats jump. The boats rocked from side to side and the Africans exchanged quick glances. It was not a human scream; it was more like a distressed animal – perhaps some kind of monkey. Or perhaps a human mimicking a monkey's cry. Some hunters were exceptionally good at this, even though there were dozens of different species found in the forest around them. They would thus draw them out of their hiding-places and then aim their poisonous spears at them, making them fall out of the trees before the rest of the troop galloped away, crying out in fear. But this cry unsettled even the four thin African rowers. Even they, who were accustomed to the sounds of the forest, found something unusual and disturbing in this scream. They paused their rowing and let the two boats float next to each other for a moment or two, as silent as twin ghosts gliding through the dusk.

"Hurry up," said the bearded man. "We haven't got all day."

The rowers did not understand the actual words barked at

them, but they comprehended the tone and resumed their rhythmic rowing.

As if out of nowhere, three crocodiles plunged into the water a short distance ahead, and made their way towards the boats, their teeth sparkling in the last rays of sunlight that touched the water. They looked as if they were smiling grimly. The rowers stopped rowing, and even the bearded man did not utter a word. Everyone sat still, but the boats kept gliding towards the crocodiles as if pulled by a magical thread. The crocodiles floated, grinning at the men advancing towards them.

"Row away, row away!" shouted the bearded man and grabbed one of the oars. Two more of his men did the same, and they all smashed the oars into the water in frantic moves, trying to get away from the crocodiles.

But the river did what rivers are meant to do and the boats continued gliding downstream, albeit hindered by the frantic rowing but advancing nonetheless straight towards the crocodiles.

As the bearded man glanced from the corner of his eye towards the shore his gaze froze – another float of five or six crocodiles lazily plunged into the water, their nostrils up in the air as if they were sensing the deliciousness of their upcoming early-evening meal.

As the two boats full of terrified men reached the float of crocodiles, the loud screams entered the shaman's consciousness as if in a dream. He put his hands on his ears, for he did not enjoy the sound of these desperate screams of men being eaten alive. As he looked into the darkening forest, a single tear dripped from the corner of his eye. Suddenly, as if by some magic trick, the evening sounds of the forest were audible to him again.

Thirty-Eight

I was sitting across from Noah at Perla in Greenwich Village. He had decided on the place.

"I don't feel comfortable in new places," he said on Tuesday. "Do you mind meeting there? I've been there several times, the food is really good. And it's a cozy place, not too big."

I didn't mind. Considering I was the one who had asked him out, I was just thrilled that I hadn't made a fool of myself.

I had come to pick Jen up from training after work, although I knew very well she was capable of getting herself home on the subway, as she had been doing every single day.

"Let's go out for dinner," I had suggested to Jen and Tom the night before. "It's been a while since we've eaten out, and the evenings are so long and warm now."

"Sure," said Jen. "Let's go to the same place we went out for your birthday, Mom. Remember that Mongolian Restaurant? I really enjoyed it."

I agreed. It was a good restaurant, but I did wonder what it would feel like to eat there just the three of us, after we visited it as a family of four on my birthday, last July, when Don and I were still together.

"I'm meeting some friends after school," said Tom. "But I can meet you at the Mongolian at seven."

"Then I'll get Jen from fencing and we'll go together," I suggested. She agreed.

The last couple of months had seen Jen turn from a frustrated teenager into a radiant fourteen-year-old. Her crush, Gabriel, had now become her first boyfriend. He asked her out a few days before her fourteenth birthday, and I was thrilled for her, even if a bit worried about what this would actually mean in her life.

But, Gabriel seemed like a totally decent young man, and he was so engrossed in his fencing and his competitions every weekend that I thought he would probably not have much time to spend with my daughter anyway.

Of course, they had fencing in common now, and Gabriel found in Jen a devoted groupie who listened for hours to his detailed descriptions about why he'd won one bout and why he'd lost another. Every point he scored was a subject for lengthy analysis, and she didn't seem to mind that.

"Gabriel can join us for dinner if you'd like," I suggested, and watched Jen's face light up. If he'd join us, we would be four again.

"Great, I'll ask him," she said.

As it turned out, Gabriel couldn't make it as he had an exam to study for. So I picked Jen up at the Manhattan Fencing Center, which is where I bumped into Noah. We hadn't spoken or seen each other since our nocturnal two-hour-long phone conversation the week before, and my heart leaped.

"Hi," he said. He'd just walked out of a coaching session, and rubbed the sweat on his forehead with his sleeve.

"Hi," I said back.

Jen walked up to join us, still wearing her fencing gear.

"Hey, are you two talking about me?" she asked.

I realized she knew nothing about our past connection.

"Jen, did you know Noah and I went to school together in San Francisco?" I asked.

She looked from me to him and back.

"No way," she said.

We both nodded, and Jen raised an eyebrow.

"Wow," she said. "What a coincidence."

"We're going out to dinner," I said to Noah. "You're welcome to join us."

I was instantly angry with myself. Where did these words come from? Was I so desperate to have a fourth person with us, not to feel as if something was missing in our lives?

Jen stared at me. I could sense her disapproval. What was I thinking, inviting one of her coaches to have dinner with us, without asking her first? She was right.

"I still have two classes to coach," said Noah. "Sorry."

"Oh, that's ok," I said, as if it didn't matter. "Another time."

"Right," said Jen, turning to leave.

"How about next Saturday?" asked Noah quietly.

Jen turned and looked at me. I looked back at her, then at Noah.

"We're at Dad's," said Jen, as if I didn't know.

Noah waited.

"Ah... yes, sure," I said. "Saturday's good."

"I'll call you later, have to get back in now," he said. "Bye, Jen."

She waved a little wave at him as he walked away, then stared at me disbelievingly. Her lips turned upwards into a thin smile.

"What?" I said.

"Nothing," she said. But she had understood.

Now Noah and I sat across from each other at Perla's, and I felt my cheeks turning red as he stared at me across the table. He had hardly said a word since we sat down, and the silence felt unnatural, as if there were things to say that were just under the surface, bubbling up slowly.

"You're very quiet today," I finally commented.

He shrugged.

"I've been told I talk too much, and that can put people off. So I'm being careful. Wouldn't want to do that. To put you off, I mean"

"Who said that?"

"My ex-wife."

"Ah," I said. I was familiar with unpleasant comments about my character coming from my ex.

"But she's right," he said. "I do talk too much, usually about fencing. It's my way to deal with the fact I don't know what to say to people. I don't do small-talk well."

"Why's that?"

"I suppose that small-talk never meant anything to me," he said. "I don't understand why people do it. What's in it for them, saying things that they don't mean, and not saying things they do mean."

That was an interesting thought. It never occurred to me that small-talk could be awkward, I always did it as part of social courtesy. But yes, he was right, it didn't make much sense when presented like that.

"But you'll happily talk about something that you're passionate about," I said.

"Yes, of course," he said. "You see, as soon as I walked into the fencing center in San Francisco for my first lesson, it was as if something had hit me on the head, or in the chest, and it wasn't a saber. It just felt right; it felt as if I had found my place in the world, because until then, I really felt as if I didn't belong. So I can always talk about fencing, that makes sense to me."

He stopped to take a breath. A waiter arrived at our table, but Noah didn't seem to notice him.

"Then," he suddenly continued, "that changed everything in my life, because I found something I was good at, and it gave me purpose. I liked to help train the younger kids."

I nodded, and smiled at the waiter who was standing patiently next to us, waiting to take our order.

"I haven't looked at the menu yet," said Noah.

"That's ok," said the young waiter. "I'll be back in a few minutes."

By the time our entrées arrived, I had heard all about his miserable teenage years, and the two fencing clubs he worked at. I understood what his ex-wife meant, but there was something endearing about his enthusiasm. He was like a small child who'd just discovered something new in the world, something he wasn't aware of before, and he was so taken with it he could just not shut up about it.

"I am sorry," he said as we started eating – he ordered a plate of sweet-potato gnocchi with cream, I ordered risotto – "Now it's your turn to talk, I want to hear all about this trip of yours to France next week."

I didn't quite know what to say – I had no problem telling him about my work-related trip, about selling French translation rights to Parisian publishers, about work lunches in French brasseries. But this would just be small-talk, wouldn't it? Could I tell him what was really going on in my mind? Could I talk about my hypnotherapy sessions that turned, involuntarily, into some strange past-life regressions? I decided to focus on eating my risotto instead, washing it down with some wonderful Pinot Grigio that the waiter poured into our glasses just before he served our plates. I noticed that Noah's glass remained untouched.

Thirty-Nine

The apprentice boy sat next to the shaman and shuffled a heap of soil from side to side with a small stick. The shaman sat in silence, his legs crossed, staring into the distance. He did not move for a long time. The boy did not dare disturb him.

Finally, the old man spoke.

"You are wondering about what happened yesterday, son."

The young man raised his eyes from the red earth and looked at the older man in expectation.

The older man put his hand out, reaching for the boy's stick. The boy handed it over.

The shaman took the stick and drew a line in the sand.

He pointed to one side of it. "This," he said, "is the side of the light. That's where we should all aim to be."

The boy stared.

"And this," said the shaman, pointing to the other side of the line, "is the side of the darkness. This is the side we should avoid."

The boy waited for the old man to continue.

"Except," he then said, "when we have no choice."

He looked the boy in the eye.

"I had no choice. I had to cross. To try and save our people. But you don't have to do that."

He drew a horizontal line across the vertical one.

"I am now here," he pointed to the side that was the side of darkness. "And once one is here, it is very difficult to cross back."

"Why?" asked the boy. "Why is it so difficult?"

The older man sighed.

"The darkness gives greater powers. It is very hard to give up power once you take it, once it takes hold of you. You can do many things with this power, and you have to be careful. It's too late for me now, but I want you to remember this, boy. Don't cross the line until you are left no choice, until someone tries to take away everything you have."

"Those men were mean," said the boy. "They deserved mean things to happen to them."

"It's not my choice," said the shaman. "I would have preferred for them to just leave us in peace. But they wouldn't. They won't. All I did was gain a little more time."

"Are they all dead?" asked the boy. "I heard the screams from the river."

The older man looked at him without blinking.

"The fate of some of them is worse than death. But the others will come back, and will bring more men with them. We have to prepare. We must keep our own people safe."

He paused for a moment, as if thinking about his next sentence.

"You have to keep your mother safe," he finally said. "We must keep her safe. You must go and hide with her in the forest; you must protect her. You now speak the language of the forest, boy."

The boy's eyes grew wide. "I don't..." he said. "Not like you, I don't know how to control the animals and..."

The shaman raised his hand. "You never control anyone," he said. "You ask for their help."

The boy nodded. "That's what I mean," he said. "I forget things."

"You will remember when you need to," said the shaman. "It will come to you. And we still have a little time. I have a little time to transmit to you my knowledge. Now I have to teach you everything you need to know."

The boy bent his head, his eyes filling with tears. "Don't send me away, please. I want to stay with you, to help you when they come back."

The shaman shook his head. "Your duty is to protect your mother, and then to be here for the others, those who will be here even after I'm gone. And it is my duty to stay here and see this through. We each have a purpose, and this is something that I knew would happen one day. I didn't know when, but I knew that this day would arrive. And it did."

The boy inched his way, closer and closer to the older man. When their knees were almost touching, the boy did something he had never done before. He put his head on the old man's shoulder. He closed his eyes, and his own shoulders started shaking as his tears wet the old man's wrinkled skin.

The shaman put his hand on the boy's head and held it there for a while, his lips quivering at first. Then a low hum made its way from the depth of his chest to his lips, and turned into a melodic chant. And this chant made its way from the hut of the shaman on the outskirts of the village up towards the darkening skies and into the forest that was bustling with life and with mystery.

Forty

I managed to fall asleep – and dream – despite the fact that the Air France flight to Paris was full, mostly with business people taking advantage of the last opportunity to travel to France before the summer holidays, when the streets of Paris turned into hot tourist-infested infernos. Early June was the very last moment to meet French publishers before they all took off for their six-week summer breaks, leaving behind only part-time secretaries and interns. I needed to speak with the bosses.

I left the kids with Don, taking one suitcase for each – full of clothes and books. And all of Jen's fencing gear, of course.

School was almost out anyway, they had done most of their exams already, but I didn't want them to have to go back home and look for things. I didn't want Don walking around my apartment when I wasn't there.

It had nothing to do with the fact Noah had spent the night, and chased away any shadows Don had left behind. I just didn't want Don there, in my space.

The Saturday night I'd spent with Noah closed the lid on the can of 'what ifs' and 'maybes' that Don had left behind. We had said we'd take a break from each other, separate for a while, and he had moved in with Claudette shortly after, as if he had only been waiting to move on.

Now, from 30,000 feet above ground, I could see why it had caused me short-term panic and anxiety. I had thought that our separation would be like a trial, a slow uphill stroll where we could support each other during our difficult moments, and let everyone adjust to the new situation. Instead, it was like a hijacking – he snatched away the freedom he just got and it was pretty clear he wasn't planning on giving it back. Not to me, anyway. It's not that I actually wanted to get back together with him, but it would have been nice to have some kind of advance warning that he'd let someone else take my place so quickly. That I was easily replaceable.

Of course, I couldn't help wonder how long this thing with Claudette had been going on, and if it had anything to do with our separation. But considering the fact that I wanted this separation – the freedom from Don – just as much as he obviously wanted the freedom from me, I had nothing to complain about. Except, I didn't move in with the first guy I met.

The memory of Noah's hands on my thighs thrilled me even now, three days after the event. His touch was gentle, slow and careful, unlike Don – who felt that twenty years of marriage gave him complete entitlement over my body.

Noah was like a child, discovering the joy of tender touch, of non-judgment, of the excitement of discovering unknown territories with a stranger. It was as if the hesitation and distance I felt during our previous encounters evaporated when we were under the sheets, and turned into confident and tender exploration.

With Jen and Tom away for the weekend it was the perfect opportunity for a bit of an adventure – and when we finished our dinner and I invited him back to my apartment, there wasn't a moment's hesitation on either side. The half bottle of cold, pale Pinot – for Noah had ordered it for me, and refrained from mentioning he did not drink but didn't want to spoil my pleasure, until it arrived at the table – helped me forget any inhabitations I had about inviting this handsome nearly-stranger back to my place. Despite the fair amount of sexual tension, we managed to keep our hands off each other in the back of the taxi.

The fifteen-minute journey back to my place was exhilarating, because I hadn't felt this kind of excitement in over twenty years, and I hadn't believed it was possible to feel it again. We were like two teenagers, holding hands, neither one of us daring to take the first step.

Until I unlocked the door, and asked him what he'd like to drink. He just stood there, looking at me, as if he didn't understand the question.

"I don't want to ruin this moment by saying something wrong," he then said, and I found his lack of self-confidence so endearing that I took his hand and led him straight to my bedroom.

Now I tried to focus on the magazines I had bought at the duty-free shop, but it wasn't easy. I took out my Kindle and tried to read something, but I kept reading the same paragraph again and again. What was up with me?

I surely couldn't be in love with Noah. He was more like an answer to all the prayers I never knew I had. It wasn't an infatuation, it was more like recognition, a realization that he had walked into my life – or drove into my life almost running me over – because the timing was right. This filled me with dread, because I had never believed in this kind of thing, in encounters that were 'meant to be'. But Noah was definitely meant to be, and I worried that perhaps it was only my wishful thinking.

Except, he said that to me, in a text message he sent me on Monday morning.

We were meant to be, he wrote. *I miss you.*

He took me to the airport after I dropped the kids off at Don's. I left my car at home and got into his familiar green Honda, the same one he almost ran me over with a month or so earlier, and listened to him speak about fencing the whole way to the airport.

"A parry in fencing is a great parallel to how people behave in real life," he said. "It's a defensive action designed to deflect an attack. It should be just wide enough to allow the attacker's blade to miss – any larger motion would be wasteful. The simplest parries move the blade in a straight line, while the more sophisticated ones move the blade diagonally, or in a circular or semicircular way. Like in life, you need to try and guess the attacker's next step. There are eight basic parries, but of course there are many derivatives of those basic eight—"

I stopped him from listing these eight and all of the derivatives by putting my hand on his thigh.

"Am I talking too much about fencing again?" he asked. "I'm sorry."

It didn't bother me at all – I wanted him to feel free to talk about whatever he wanted. I, for once, didn't feel the need to say anything, just to listen. He was like a piece of a puzzle that had clicked into my life, making me – if not complete – then at least larger and more comfortable than I had been before he arrived. As if his sudden appearance in my life had allowed me to expand.

I had four more hours before landing in Paris, and as my thoughts about Noah prevented me from reading, and from working, I decided to try and sleep some more.

Forty-One

When the men came back, the villagers were ready for them. Or as ready as they could be.

Ten boats made their way up the river that morning, right past *that spot*. They looked at it in silence and some of the Portuguese men shook their heads.

They pointed at the riverbanks and looked around in fear, but there were no crocodiles in sight. Burying their compatriots' remains was not a pleasant job, and they did not want to share their fate.

The Africans kept rowing silently past *that spot* and onto the place where the men silently disembarked, carrying their muskets solemnly. They grouped together and talked in hushed voices, but the wind carried the sounds all the way to the village, to the shaman's hut.

When the wind brought him their voices, he gathered his few belongings and left them all in one corner of the hut, as if packing for a voyage. He then put on a birdlike headdress made of cloth and feathers and tied on his best garment – a large, elaborately decorated cape – both left to him by his father, and by his grandfather before him, and picked up his cane.

Slowly, without any haste, he shuffled his feet on the dusty path toward the village. The village men were already waiting, their faces painted and their arrows dipped in poison. Small branches were tied to their hair, giving them an intimidating, inhuman appearance. The dark black circles painted under their eyes were expertly smudged with soft bird feathers, and the war-red on their high cheekbones and dark forehand shone like fresh blood. They waited silently in a shady, nearby enclave of the forest, chewing on some roots that were to give them strength, as well as enhance their night vision.

The shaman walked slowly towards them and blessed each and every warrior by quietly chanting and waving his hands over their heads, wishing upon them the swiftness of monkeys and the strength of lions.

The group slowly dispersed, gliding into the forest silently. The shaman was left on his own, and started shuffling his feet towards the center of the village, towards the baobab tree stump. As he passed the village huts he called out and tapped his cane.

"Anyone still here?" he called. "Is everyone gone? They are coming!"

There was no answer, no movement around him.

He had hoped that all the women and children were well-hidden in the forest, and all the men well-armed, their arrows dipped in deadly poison, waiting for their opponents to come nearer.

He then arrived at the baobab stump and sat by it, leaning his back against its comforting trunk.

Forty-Two

The Paris meetings were as expected – some successful, some less so. I sold the French translation and distribution rights for twelve of our books, which more than made my trip worthwhile. It was all a whirlwind of business lunches, after-work drinks on the terraces of French cafés in the late-afternoon Parisian breeze and in between, some negotiations in stuffy Parisian offices. The French seemed to have their own way of conducting business: small-talk followed by sudden and ruthless discussions straight to the point. I couldn't help thinking of Noah and his dislike of small-talk, but his passion with parries. I could see his point about how they could be representative of real life.

"The trick with counter parry-ripostes, and all fencing," he had said, "is to maintain your composure. You never know exactly what your opponent is planning, although you can sometimes guess by watching them before the bout, while fencing against another opponent. But the wisest thing is to stay calm and deliberate for as long as possible."

I used this technique in my negotiations with the agents and editors in Paris, and I was surprised by how well it worked every single time. The mindfulness in fencing, that same mindfulness Noah must have mentioned ten times in the two days we spent together, worked in my favor when used in business.

I suddenly got what he was talking about; I really got it. I watched my opponents across the table, tried to guess what they were about to say or do, and did my best to stay calm. Then I made my verbal counterattack, which often caught them off guard.

I wanted to call Noah and thank him, but knew he rarely answered his cellphone. It was off most of the time as he was coaching. It was late afternoon in Paris, mid-morning in New York, so I texted him: *Your parry-riposte technique works in business too.*

The reply was almost immediate: *Of course it does. I miss you.*

The tenderness that came through in this short message brought tears to my eyes – I had not experienced such a simple and honest display of emotions for so many years. Yet I felt uncomfortable returning it. I had been conditioned to keep my feelings bottled up for so long. My fingers hesitated over my blackberry keyboard, and I finally typed: *Off to the Pays de Gex tomorrow morning to complete research.*

Enjoy he typed back.

None of the negative comments I got from Don about my novel, about my writing, about my personality and about my life. How refreshing.

Well, it's a new relationship, I tried to justify it to myself. *Let's see what happens in a few weeks with all of this.*

The three-hour train-ride from the Gare de Lyon in Paris to the Cornavin train-station in central Geneva was relaxing. I just sat back and thought of nothing in particular, letting the sweet feeling of anticipation fill my being. There was a lot of anticipation – of the upcoming adventure in a place I had been to only in my dreams, anticipation for what I would discover there, anticipation of going back home and seeing what the relationship with Noah might bring, how it might develop.

As I got off at the train-station in Geneva and looked for a taxi to Gex, I felt my legs could hardly support me. The taxi driver, who offered to take my suitcase out of my hand and put it in the trunk of his car, must have thought I was not in my right mind.

"Everything ok, *madame*?"

"Yes, thank you," I mumbled and landed with a thump in the back seat of his silver-gray Audi.

I had the most peculiar feeling of recognition: I'd definitely been there before. Even the smell in the air was familiar, although I could not say how.

As soon as we left the city and crossed the border into neighboring France, green fields and the rolling foothills of the Jura replaced the concrete-gray of Geneva.

Something inside me clicked, as if I had suddenly become another person, a fuller one, a multidimensional being rather than the woman, mother, wife and then ex-wife I was so used to being. I knew no one who I could share this feeling with, for it didn't make sense to me either. It was more than a déjà vu. It was an expansion.

As the taxi approached the small town of Gex, at the foothills of the Jura, I felt almost nauseous with excitement.

The driver made some comments about Gex and the surrounding area, as if I were a tourist, a foreigner in this town, and he were my tour guide.

"Zis is the town that gave its name to the Pays de Gex," he said, insisting to speak to me in English, despite the fact I spoke pretty decent French, albeit with an American accent. "In the early 19th century it was placed in the customs region of Switzerland and given a neutral status, but the treaty of Versailles, how do you say? Cancelled this decision. Everybody wanted this town."

"Right," I said. I just wanted to be able to watch the cobbled streets, to look for something familiar. Nothing actually looked as if I'd seen it before, but something was… Something inside me told me I had in fact been here before, many times.

As the taxi stopped in front of the small hotel I'd booked on the Internet while still in New York, and the driver took my suitcase out of the trunk, I fumbled for some money in my wallet. The meter showed seventy – but seventy what?

On the Swiss side, at the train station, they used Swiss francs. But here, on the French side, a mere twenty-minute drive from Geneva, the currency was euros. I asked the driver what he'd prefer. He replied that he'd accept either – it didn't matter, although euros were worth slightly more than Swiss francs these days.

I gave him seventy euros and asked him to keep the change. That seemed to make him happy, and he shook my hand enthusiastically.

"*Merci*, enjoy your visit here. If you need a taxi again, here is my card. My name is Yves Bais," he said as he handed me a card. "And you are, Madame...?"

"Adele Durand," I said as I accepted the card and thanked him.

Only after he drove off, I realized what I had actually said.

Forty-Three

I woke up dripping with sweat. I then looked around and realized where I was – at the small hotel in Gex, across from the cinema. The Hotel Bellevue. The room was stuffy and dusty, and I got out of bed to open the window. As I looked outside at the silent, cobbled streets, I tried to hold on to the disappearing threads of my nightmare. It was the shaman again.

The Portuguese men came to the village early in the morning. Most of the village women and children had spent the night in the forest, but the men stayed behind, to defend their village.

The Portuguese men marched to the center of the village, and found one old man in traditional dress sitting silently by the stump of the baobab tree. He looked like an ancient, tired bird, his headdress made of large feathers carefully and elaborately worked into a cloth that covered his head and most of his face. They'd never seen anything like it.

"Where is everyone?" they barked at him, but he didn't answer. He just chanted, staring straight through them with his dark eyes.

Without a word, they shot him. He collapsed on the ground in silence, like an empty bag of wheat, as if the bones in his body had turned into dust. He bled into the ground, the red liquid turning the earth around him black.

The chanting stopped and the Portuguese men were relieved; it was as if the energy had shifted, become clearer.

Then the poisonous spears and arrows started hitting them from all directions – from beyond the huts, from the trees above them, and they responded with explosive gunshots. Men dropped from the trees as if they were dead birds, bodies covered the red earth in even more patches of dark blood.

They spared the lives of some young men, whom they chained to each other and pulled towards the river.

Three of the Portuguese men stayed behind, checking each and every hut to make sure there was no one else left to kill, or to take as slave.

Then they set fire to a few of the huts, just to teach the stubborn natives a lesson. They realized that the women and children would return – but they weren't interested in them, not just yet. They might come back for more slaves in a fortnight.

No one bothered to check the shaman's hut, on the outskirts of the village, where there was one last young man hiding, numb with fear. It was the shaman's apprentice, the only survivor of the cruel massacre.

I touched my cheeks and they were wet with tears. Why did I need to come all the way to this small French town to learn of the cruel ending of the shaman's life? It was a sad and senseless death, a tragic end to a lonely life. Yet I was full of respect towards the old man, who did his best to improve the fate of his people, and failed. He showed only kindness to the deaf-dumb woman, and to her son. And although he'd crossed the lines between magic and sorcery, he was never evil. He was good.

The dream felt so real, I had no doubt that I somehow was connected to a sad and terrible period in history, the early years of the slave trade in Africa. Yet, I did not feel personally involved in this story, it was not like Adele's tale. Who was this shaman, and who was his apprentice? I felt great tenderness, sadness and love for them both. As if they were family members I deeply cared about.

When I looked at my watch I realized it was four a.m. I quickly calculated it would be ten p.m. in New York City. I could not sleep anymore; this nightmare shook me deeply. I turned the light on and looked for the Blackberry in my handbag.

I'll send a message to Noah, I thought. I wanted to connect with him, to try and get out of my shell and express how much I was missing him. The terrible nightmare made me feel emotional and raw, and the only person who might be able to understand me right now was him.

As I looked at my phone, I saw a text message there. It was a quote.

Be soft, it said. *Do not let the world make you hard. Do not let pain make you hate. Do not let the bitterness steal your sweetness. Take pride that even though the rest of the world may disagree, you still believe it to be a beautiful place. ~ Kurt Vonnegut.*

It was from Noah.

How did he know I needed comforting just now, so early in the morning in France?

Thank you so much for your message, I typed. *Just had a terrible nightmare.*

There was no reply; perhaps he had already gone to bed.

I decided to get dressed and take an early-morning walk, explore the cobbled streets in the pre-dawn silence, before they awoke to the hectic morning of what was now a dormitory town of Geneva – people getting into their cars and driving twenty or thirty minutes to their workplaces in the city.

As I walked up the street towards the *boulangerie*, which was the only place to have its light on at five a.m., I thought I could recognize the place where Adele – or was it I? – had stepped off the carriage in one of my very first dreams of her, or perhaps it was in a regression with Tatiana, I could not differentiate between the two anymore. But I could now vividly remember how the carriage stopped and two women gathered their skirts and stepped down into the street, the very street I was now standing in.

"*Merci*, Monsieur Garnier," said the older of the two women. "Please meet us here in about three hours, to take us home."

"*Oui, Madame Durand, bien sûr,*" said the carriage driver and cracked his whip to prompt his horse to gallop off.

The younger of the two women stood there, where I stood now, her heart full of hope and of thoughts of a new dress, and of the love she felt for the schoolteacher that I – Amelia – now knew that she would never marry in that lifetime.

Forty-Four

Now that memories started flowing in like a river of information, I remembered something else. I remembered there was another place that had appeared in my regressions, and in my dreams. It was a place called Chevry, where Adele's home had been. It was not difficult to find out that it was five miles to the south of Gex. I figured I could try and take the bus there. However, a short investigation revealed that the buses were infrequent and the signaling was totally unclear. Even with my more-than-decent French, I could not figure it out.

I could try to walk there – it would probably take me over an hour to walk five miles, maybe two hours if I took it slowly. This was the walk that the schoolteacher took to go and visit Adele every weekend, from Gex to Chevry and back, and I wanted to walk it with my own two feet, like some sort of strange pilgrimage to another lifetime.

I thanked my good sense for having packed a pair of comfortable shoes as well as the necessary high heels I wore for my business meetings in Paris. After sipping a cup of strong coffee and enjoying two croissants in the hotel's breakfast room, I headed out towards Chevry.

"Sure, there are some footpaths, but there is a lot of overgrowth," said the hotel matron as an answer to my question, as she served my coffee.

"Nobody walks these paths anymore. Two hundred years ago it was the only way if you didn't have your own horse and carriage, but today everyone has cars. Except the teenagers, who hitchhike. Unfortunately the bus service around here is not very reliable. One thing that still needs improvement."

It was a bright morning, and the sun was warm but merciful

as I followed the main road to Chevry. The walk was slightly uphill at first, the Jura mountain range to my right, the sun to my left.

I loved walking, and as much as walking in New York City was nice, walking across the fields full of small yellow flowers, with the occasional hare or rabbit (for I admit to not knowing the difference) scurrying away, was simply divine.

An occasional car drove by, but no one stopped to offer me a ride. They must have just assumed I was some strange woman on a morning stroll along the road between the town of Gex and the village of Chevry, which wasn't very far from the truth.

It took me just over ninety minutes to walk to Chevry, at a good pace. How fast did the schoolteacher walk, accompanied by his dog, when he went to see Adele? He must have really wanted to see her, if he made the effort of taking this journey every Sunday. And then, his disappointment of her marrying that merchant from Gex... I didn't want to think of it, as it caused me physical pain, a big lump in my throat.

I was surprised to feel tears rolling down my cheeks as I walked, thinking of the sad life, the bad decision Adele had made. Or perhaps it was not a bad decision? Maybe it was just a learning experience, a lesson she needed to learn? One way or another, I knew Adele had regretted that decision, for I could feel the regret in the pit of my stomach as I approached Chevy.

Chevry was a lovely small village, with an upper part signposted Chevry Dessus and a lower part, Chevry Dessous. I chose to turn left, to the lower part of the village. It seemed like there was more going on there – a church, a small city hall, some interesting-looking houses. I walked around as if I was moonstruck. It was all unfamiliar, yet familiar at the same time. It all looked different, yet I had no doubt that I'd been here before.

I stopped at the only place I could see – a small café – to have a glass of freshly-squeezed orange juice. It tasted heavenly after the long walk. The gray-haired gentleman behind the bar was busy with his morning paper, and after serving me the juice, together with a small piece of paper – the check for three euros – stuck his nose back in the paper and ignored me.

I drank my juice, left a few coins and continued my stroll in this strange little village. I closed my eyes and enjoyed the sudden breeze that blew through the courtyard of the church as I passed it, and let my feet take me where they seemed to want to go – uphill. And so, I found myself in the upper part of Chevry – Chevry Dessus – and on the Rue du Chateau. I loved looking at old chateaux and I decided to see whether I could walk in and have a look – I was in luck, as the gates were open. A small sign indicated that this chateau had belonged to the Baron Girod de l'Ain in the nineteenth century, but that the building was older than that – circa 1700. When was Adele around, if she was even real?

"Of course she was," said a voice in my head. *"She was no more and no less real than you are."*

For the first time, I really listened to this voice.

I continued wandering through the small chateau – no one seemed to be there but me – which I found to be strange, almost surreal.

I touched the ancient cold walls, running my fingers over the stones, reading the small commemorative plaques that were everywhere.

Until I got to one that stopped me in my tracks; that took my breath away. It was under a display of ancient swords, most of them dark and rusty – but still impressive with the power and the energy they held. And the plaque read:

En memoire de Jules Badeau, enseignant et maître d'armes, 1745-1807.

I felt as if I was going to faint. I had to hold on to the wall to stay upright.

Just then, I heard feet shuffling, and an elderly woman walked into the room.

"Bonjour, madame," she said cheerfully but then she approached quickly and held on to me as she saw I was shaking.

"Vous n'etes pas bien, madame?" she asked, and all I could do was shake my head and point at the plaque. *In memory of Jules Badeau, teacher and master of arms.* And those years, just looking at them sent shivers down my spine. 1745 to 1807. This man, Jules Badeau, this schoolteacher of my dreams, actually existed – over two hundred years ago.

The woman nodded.

"Oui, he was a great man, they say he was the first to bring fencing, *escrime,* from the big city, Lyon to this small village. He taught many boys, including the boys of the family who owned this chateau. When it was bought and turned into a museum, they decided to leave all these displays up here."

"But..."

There was nothing I could say. Nothing that I could think, or imagine, which could explain this. The old woman just stared at me, baffled.

There was no way I could walk back to Gex, my legs were shaking, my head spinning. I sat down on a stone bench while the woman brought me a glass of water, then called her son, who drove me back to my small hotel in Gex, a mere ten-minute drive.

"Will you be all right, *madame?"* he asked as he dropped me off at reception, and all I could do was thank him and nod. Then I went up to my room, lay on my bed, and cried like I had never cried in my entire life – tears of pain, of sorrow, of regret, but also, in some strange way – tears of relief.

Forty-Five

That evening I called Noah on his cellphone, and he answered on the second ring.

"I hoped you'd call," he said.

He'd replied to my message about the nightmare from that morning with another tender, loving message, and I felt that I wanted to take the risk of connecting with him – a connection that felt deeper than any other romantic relationship I had ever had, my twenty-something-year marriage included.

"Why's that?"

Now, at the sound of his voice, I felt I was almost back to my confident self. I could tease him a little.

He hesitated. "You wrote you had a nightmare. I feel for you, because I have them often, especially in the last few years. Especially since my divorce three years ago."

Again, he disarmed me with his straightforward honesty. With all of his Aspergerian behavior and social difficulties, what an uncomplicated man he was. Much easier to understand and relate to than the overconfident, ever-smiling Don.

"What are your nightmares about?" I asked.

Again, he hesitated.

"Tell me yours and I'll tell you mine," I added, as if I was back to being a teenager.

"I am dying," he says. "Every single time, it's the same death."

I waited for more.

"I am alone in the forest, surrounded by a group of men," he said. "I am African. They are white. They are scared of me, yet they are violent. They shout at me, I don't understand their words. But I feel their anger, their evil vibes."

I held my breath.

"I feel a huge amount of pain," he said. "Not in real life, but in the dream. I feel lonely, sad, but also resigned to a coming death. And then it's over. They shoot me; they shoot me as if I were nothing to them. They shoot me every single time. And then I wake up, and there's sadness and pain all around me. I don't understand this dream, this nightmare, but it's always the same one."

I felt numb again, my panic from earlier on now compounded, by this even stranger synchronicity. Stranger than anything else that had happened to me in my entire life.

I didn't know what to say.

"What was yours about?" he then asked.

Now it was my turn to hesitate. Could I really tell him?

"You said you'd tell me," he said, as if reading my mind.

"The same thing," I said.

"Same thing as what?"

"Same thing as you," I said. "An African man being killed by a group of white men. Terrible, violent men, looking to take slaves from the old man's village."

He remained silent for a few moments.

"Really?" he finally said. "You're joking, right?"

"No, I am not," I said. "But it's the first time I've had this dream, this nightmare. Although I've been dreaming about this African man for a while now. But last night, this morning, I dreamt that he was murdered by a bunch of white men. Something like the beginning of the slave trade. They were looking to take young people from his village as slaves, and he was protecting them. He was some kind of medicine man, a shaman."

I heard a quiet, low laughter on the other end of the line.

"Shaman," he said. "Probably not a very easygoing fellow."

"Probably not," I said.

"So, if this was me, if it was like a past life or something, it would explain my social difficulties, wouldn't it?" He tried to laugh it off, although I could sense he was tense.

"I guess it could, if this was like a past life," I said. *Or something*, I thought.

We both remained silent, the distance across the Atlantic Ocean disappearing. I felt as if we were together, in the same room.

"There's something I really don't understand about this connection we have," he said. "Do you feel it too?"

I didn't know how to answer that.

"Noah," I finally said, "I am leaving here tomorrow, arriving back in New York on Wednesday."

"I know," he said.

"Are you free on Wednesday evening?" I asked. "I think we have a lot to talk about."

"I am free on Wednesday evening," he said.

"It's not that I don't miss my kids, but I'll pick them up on Friday," I said. "It's good for them to spend some time with Don. They're probably fine, right?"

"I saw Jen at the club yesterday, her dad brought her. She looked her usual happy self," he said. "I'll check on her tomorrow, she normally trains on Tuesdays after school. I won't say you're coming back on Wednesday."

"So you think it's a good idea to pick them up on Friday? It'll give us a day or two to…"

"I think it's a very good idea."

"Thank you, Noah. I miss them, it's just that… I need to sort out some stuff in my head first."

"Can I try to help you sort it out?" he asked, and all I wanted to do was be near him.

"I would like you to," I said. "I really would".

Neither of us wanted to hang up, but in the end we did. And I fell into a deep sleep that lasted nearly ten hours, and the next morning when I woke up, packed and checked out of the hotel, I knew I'd be back in Gex again, in the not-too-distant future.

I didn't know if I'd be able to tell Noah what I'd been through, if I'd find the right words, if I'd find the courage. I didn't want to alienate him, to scare him off. I wanted, with all my heart, for our relationship to work.

But I knew that even more than that, I wanted to bring him here, and then take him to the small chateau of Chevry, show him the plaque and watch his reaction, without saying a word. Just letting the realization, perhaps even the recognition, sink in. And then drive him back to the small hotel in Gex and try to make up for everything.

For readers and book clubs
Q&A with Daniela I. Norris

The characters in *Recognitions* are intertwined although they live in different eras and are of different ages and backgrounds. Did you find it difficult to connect between them?

I found that the connection between the characters of Amelia, a modern-day editor from New York, and Adele, a young woman from eighteenth-century France, came quite naturally. In fact, I first wrote the story of Adele, then the shaman, then the story of Amelia. After the three threads were written, it was like braiding a plait.

How is the shaman connected to Adele and Amelia?

This is a very good question and a great discussion point: one I am still in the process of answering myself as I am now writing the sequel to *Recognitions*, titled *Premonitions*. The shaman's character was there all along, and he is very important in both the lives of Adele, and of Amelia. He is like a shadow following them from one life to another. He is an important part of who they are and who they will become.

Can you say more about the sequel?

It is hard to talk about something that is still in the making; it's like a daydream unfolding in my mind. But I do plan a trilogy, with *Recognitions* being the first book, and *Premonitions* the second.

The characters in *Recognitions* seem to have specific roles in each other's lives, do you think that people really have prede-

termined roles in other people's lives?

I don't know if people have predetermined roles in others' lives, but I always believed that some people act as 'flags' in the lives of others. Someone, often a stranger, can get us to do something or help us avoid doing something as if by chance – and then disappear from our lives. I believe it could be because their role in our lives was specific, punctual. Of course, there are others who might have much larger, more dominant roles in our lives. Others yet will accompany us on longer stretches of our lives' journeys.

You are a former diplomat, how does this affect your writing?

Many people wonder how someone who was into politics and international affairs for many years can turn to spiritual or inspirational writing – for me it is quite obvious. Politics keep us grounded, living in the here and now. Spiritual or inspirational writings can uplift us; can help us make this world a better place. One without the other would be difficult for many people, as not many of us can live in a spiritual bubble or in a monastery at the top of the world. Most of us need to live in the real world, and trying to see the 'bigger picture' through spirituality while keeping a tab on world events is, in my opinion, a healthy combination.

What are the themes of this upcoming trilogy?

I'd love to be able to write about the themes of past lives, or even life-between-lives, in an interesting and grounded sort of way. I don't see myself as a 'new age' writer, I see myself as a writer who is interested in many things, and my books are just a reflection of these interests.

How can readers learn more about theories of past lives or even life-between-lives?

There are many good researchers and writers out there who have published some fantastic books in the last thirty years or so. Namely – Dr. Brian Weiss, Dr. Michael Newton, Andy Tomlinson, Michael E. Tymn, David Fontana, Stafford Betty and many others. Their books are certainly worth reading if you want to learn more about these concepts. Different religions such as Buddhism, Hinduism and the Druze (an ethno-religious esoteric group) also have some fascinating writings and theories about those topics. These could be a great starting point.

Anything else you'd like to share with your readers?

It feels like I've shared a lot of my beliefs in *Recognitions* and in this Q&A session. I just want readers to know that I never try to convince anyone of anything. You don't have to believe in past lives to enjoy a good story, which is hopefully what I managed to achieve in this book, and will continue to achieve in the trilogy.

I don't want readers to feel as if spirituality or the topic of past lives are being imposed on them – they are merely offered as one possible explanation to experiences many of us have in our lives.

Lastly, please take a few moments to leave a review of *Recognitions* on Amazon or other websites. Reviews really help authors. It doesn't have to be long or gushing, it can be just one or two honest sentences. They will be much appreciated.

Acknowledgements

This novel is the product of my imagination, combined with past-life regressions and research. All resemblance to people, dead or alive is – naturally – purely coincidental.

It is also the result of inspiration provided by many people:

The team at John Hunt Publishing – the inspiring John Hunt, awesome editor Dominic C. James and the wonderful Maria Barry, Catherine Harris, Nick Welch, Stuart Davies, Mary Flatt, Sarah Dedman.

Four writing divas and friends – Katie Hayoz, Amanda Callendrier, Paula Read and Jawahara Saidullah, I appreciate your support and insights while working on *Recognitions*.

Susan Tiberghien – author, teacher, mentor and founder of the Geneva Writers' Group – who always continues to inspire.

Teachers and friends from the Regression Academy in the UK – Andy Tomlinson, Wissam Awad, Tatjana Radovanovic, Hazel Newton, Janet Treloar, Bel Rogers and others too many to name here – thanks for helping me understand.

Maitres d'Armes Yannick Sumac, Eric Desperier, George Hadzopoulos, Thomas Drouet and Jon Salfield– who are not only masters of arms but also of knowing what motivates and inspires young fencers.

Julia Gelman from the Manhattan Fencing Center.

Lior Bar-On, translator, friend and Asperger expert.

My beta readers – fencer Vittoria Tomich, fellow International Grief Council panelist Lo Anne Mayer, Siara Isaac, Anne Webber – thank you for helping make *Recognitions* a better book with your insights and thoughts. I am grateful to you all.

My mother Irina and two fathers – Harry and Ramy – you are the best. And my three brothers – Daniel, Gabriel and Michael – two on this side of life and one on the other – I love you all, and always will.

Last but certainly not least – my husband Richard and sons

Roman, Adam and Aramis – I know that we are not together just by chance; we are together to learn from each other, for better or for worse. Thank you for accompanying me on my life journey.

Daniela I. Norris, Geneva, 2015

About the Author

Daniela I. Norris is a former diplomat, turned writer. She is the author of two non-fiction books (*Crossing Qalandiya*, Reportage Press, 2010; *On Dragonfly Wings*, Axis Mundi, 2014) and one collection of short stories (*Collecting Feathers*, Soul Rocks, 2014).

She lives with her family near Geneva, Switzerland, where she is very much involved with the Geneva Writers' Group and is the co-director of the Geneva Writers' Conference. Her stories and articles have won awards and have been published in magazines and anthologies.

Following the unexpected and sudden death of her younger brother Michael in 2010, Daniela's writing shifted from political to spiritual, as a result of her training as a hypnotherapist, specializing in Past-Lives and Life-Between-Lives Regression Therapy. She is also a member of the International Grief Council (www.internationalgriefcouncil.org) as well as the founder of the website and spiritual hub www.tweetsfromtheafterlife.com

Recognitions is her first novel.

Also from John Hunt Publishing by Daniela I. Norris

Collecting Feathers: Tales from The Other Side

In *Collecting Feathers*, Daniela I. Norris blends pitch-perfect story-telling and a keen spiritual awareness to bring us a beautiful and haunting set of tales from the beyond. A feast for the heart, mind and soul, each story is layered with unfolding intrigue, and each one will stay with you long after the pages have been turned.

'Birth, death, afterbirth and afterlife are all intricately wind together against the backdrop of tragedies happening daily and how people cope, move on, and move outward. That's the living, breathing, beating heart of *Collecting Feathers*, especially recommended not for those who expect entertainment from their short stories, but for readers more interested in reflective pieces spiced with poetic imagery and succinct (but striking) revelations.'
Diane Donovan, Midwest Book Review

'Here we have eleven short stories which are very gently ghostly. Not a book for the horror fan these tales are mostly uplifting accounts of contact written from a medium's perception of the Inner Planes.'
The Inner Light, Vol 35, No 1

On Dragonfly Wings: a skeptic's journey to mediumship

On Dragonfly Wings – a Skeptic's Journey to Mediumship, is a candid and personal search for the meaning of life, of death and of grief. It aims to give hope to those who have lost a loved one and to those who are about to pass beyond – hope that this is not an end. Written for lay people, rather than experienced spiritualists or mediums, and for anyone who is curious about exploring further, it provides practical tools to help readers find their own spiritual truth and path.

'Based on the experiences of the author, upon the untimely death of her brother, it is a well-written and engaging story with plenty of evidence to give comfort to the bereaved.'
Kindred Spirit Magazine

'As a consultant in mediumship, I would say it brings the subject to a wider audience in a relevant, no nonsense and demystifying way.'
Rosemary H. C. Hudson, BSc, Society of Women Writers and Journalists

'The reader who is grieving the loss of a loved one or who is simply looking for the path leading toward a more meaningful life should find much to ponder on in this very interesting book.'
Michael E. Tymn

At Roundfire we publish great stories. We lean towards the spiritual and thought-provoking. But whether it's literary or popular, a gentle tale or a pulsating thriller, the connecting theme in all Roundfire fiction titles is that once you pick them up you won't want to put them down.